ALSO BY HISHAM MATAR

In the Country of Men

ANATOMY OF A

DISAPPEARANCE

ANATOMY OF A DISAPPEARANCE

A Novel

HISHAM MATAR

THE DIAL PRESS NEW YORK

Copyright © 2011 by Hisham Matar

Published in the United States by The Dial Press,
an imprint of The Random House Publishing Group,
a division of Random House, Inc., New York.

DIAL PRESS is a registered trademark of Random House, Inc.,
and the colophon is a trademark of Random House, Inc.

Portions of this book appeared previously in *The New Yorker* in different form.

Originally published in hardcover in the United Kingdom by Viking,
an imprint of Penguin Books, Penguin Books Ltd.

Library of Congress Cataloging-in-Publication Data
Matar, Hisham.
Anatomy of a disappearance : a novel / Hisham Matar.
p. cm.
ISBN 978-0-385-34044-1
eBook ISBN 978-0-679-64398-2
1. Fathers and sons—Fiction. 2. Missing persons—Fiction. 3. Family secrets—
Fiction. 4. Stepmothers—Fiction. 5. Cairo (Egypt)—Fiction. I. Title.
PR6113.A87A84 2011
823'.92—dc22   2011001561

Printed in the United States of America on acid-free paper

www.dialpress.com

2 4 6 8 9 7 5 3 1

First U.S. Edition

Book design by Caroline Cunningham

Title page image by Julia Soboleva

To J.H.M.

ANATOMY OF A

DISAPPEARANCE

CHAPTER 1

There are times when my father's absence is as heavy as a child sitting on my chest. Other times I can barely recall the exact features of his face and must bring out the photographs I keep in an old envelope in the drawer of my bedside table. There has not been a day since his sudden and mysterious vanishing that I have not been searching for him, looking in the most unlikely places. Everything and everyone, existence itself, has become an evocation, a possibility for resemblance. Perhaps this is what is meant by that brief and now almost archaic word: elegy.

I do not see him in the mirror but feel him adjusting, as if he were twisting within a shirt that nearly fits. My father has always been intimately mysterious even when he was present. I can almost imagine how it might have been coming to him as an equal, as a friend, but not quite.

× × ×

My father disappeared in 1972, at the beginning of my school Christmas holiday, when I was fourteen. Mona and I were staying at the Montreux Palace, taking breakfast— I with my large glass of bright orange juice, and she with her steaming black tea—on the terrace overlooking the steel-blue surface of Lake Geneva, at the other end of which, beyond the hills and the bending waters, lay the now vacant city of Geneva. I was watching the silent paragliders hover above the still lake, and she was paging through *La Tribune de Genève*, when suddenly her hand rose to her mouth and trembled.

A few minutes later we were aboard a train, hardly speaking, passing the newspaper back and forth.

We collected from the police station the few belongings that were left on the bedside table. When I unsealed the small plastic bag, along with the tobacco and the lighter flint, I smelled him. That same watch is now wrapped round my wrist, and even today, after all these years, when I press the underside of the leather strap against my nostrils I can detect a whiff of him.

× × ×

I wonder now how different my story would have been were Mona's hands unbeautiful, her fingertips coarse.

I still, all of these years later, hear the same childish persistence, "I saw her first," which bounced like a devil on my tongue whenever I caught one of Father's claiming gestures: his fingers sinking into her hair, his hand landing on her skirted thigh with the absentmindedness of a man touching his earlobe in mid-sentence. He had taken to the Western habit of holding hands, kissing, embracing in public. But he could not fool me; like a bad actor, he seemed unsure of his steps. Whenever he would catch me watching him, he would look away and I swear I could see color in his cheeks. A dark tenderness rises in me now as I think how hard he had tried; how I yearn still for an easy sympathy with my father. Our relationship lacked what I have always believed possible, given time and perhaps after I had become a man, after he had seen me become a father: a kind of emotional eloquence and ease. But now the distances that had then governed our interactions and cut a quiet gap between us continue to shape him in my thoughts.

CHAPTER 2

We met Mona at the Magda Marina, a small hotel in Alexandria's Agamy Beach. Although the sea was nearby, we did not swim in it and I never asked to build sand castles. Most of the guests, too, ignored it and were content with the shelter and limited pleasures of the swimming pool. The concrete-box structures of the single-story rooms screened us from the surrounding landscape. You could hear the waves lapping lazily against the shore like a snoring guard dog, but we caught only narrow glimpses of the blueness.

Father had been bringing me here for the past two summers, ever since Mother's sudden passing.

We never came to places such as the Magda Marina when my mother was alive. She did not like the heat. I never saw her in a swimsuit or in sudden surrender closing her eyes at the sun. The coming of Cairene spring would set her off planning our summer getaways. Once we summered high up in the Swiss Alps, where my body stiffened at the sight of deep, hollow chasms emptied out of the rocky earth.

Another time she took us to Nordland in northern Norway, where austere black mountains reflected sharply their splintered peaks on the unmoving waters. We stayed in a wooden cabin that stood alone by the water and was painted the brown-red of withered leaves. Round its roof hung a gutter as wide as a human thigh. Here whatever fell from the sky fell in abundance. There was no other man-made structure in sight. Some afternoons Mother disappeared, and I would not let on to Father that my heart was thumping at the base of my ears. I would keep to my room until I heard footsteps on the deck then the kitchen door slide open. Once I found her there with hands stained black-red, a rough globe dyed into the front of her sweater. With eyes as clean as glass, wide, satisfied, she held out a handful of wild berries. They tasted of a ripe sweetness I found hard to attribute to that landscape.

One night fog gathered thickly, abstracting the licks and sighs of the northern lights. You need adulthood to appreciate such horror. An anxious heat entered my eight-year-old mind, and I curled up in bed, trying to muffle the crying, hoping Mother would pay me one of her night visits, kiss my forehead, lie beside me. In the morning the still world returned: the innocent waters, the ferocious mountains, the pale sky dotted with small, newborn clouds. I found her in the kitchen, warming milk, a glass of water standing on the white marble counter beside her. Not juice, tea, coffee, but water was her morning drink. She took a sip and with her usual insistence on soundlessness muffled the impact with the soft tip of her little finger. Any sudden sound unsettled her. She could conduct an entire day's chores in near silence. I sat at the rented table where, when the three of us gathered at mealtimes, Mother would occasionally glance at the fourth empty chair as if it signaled an absence, something lost. She poured the hot milk. A sliver of steam brushed the air then disappeared beside her neck.

"Why the long face?" she said.

She took me out onto the deck that stretched above the lake. The air was so brisk it stung my throat. We stood in silence. I remembered what she had said to Father in the car when the naked mountains of Nordland first came into view: "Here God decided to be a sculptor; everywhere else He holds back."

"Holds back?" Father had echoed. "You talk about Him as if He's a friend of yours."

In those days Father did not believe in God. He often greeted Mother's remembrances of the Divine with irritated sarcasm. Perhaps I should not have been surprised when, after Mother died, he would now and again voice a prayer; sarcasm, more often than not, hides a secret fascination.

× × ×

Was it the romance of wood fires, the discretion of heavy coats, that attracted my mother to the north and unpeopled places of Europe? Or was it the impeccable stillness of a fortnight spent mostly sheltered indoors with the only two people she could lay claim to? I have come to think of those holidays, no matter where they were, as having taken place in a single country—her country—and the silences that marked them her melancholy. There were moments when her unhappiness seemed as elemental as clear water.

After she died it soon became obvious that what Father had always wanted to do, in the two weeks he allowed himself off every summer, was to lie in the sun all day. So the Magda Marina became the place where he and I spent that fortnight. He seemed to have lost his way with me; widowhood had dispossessed him of any ease that he had once had around his only child. When we sat down to eat he either read the paper or gazed into the distance. Whenever he noticed me looking at him he would fidget or check his watch. As soon as he had finished eating he would light a cigarette and snap his fingers for the bill, not bothering to see whether I had finished too.

"See you back in the room."

He never did that when Mother was alive.

Instead, when the three of us went to a restaurant, they would sit side by side facing me. If we were all engaged in some conversation she would direct most of her contributions toward me, as if I were the front wall of a squash court. And when his unease led him to play the entertainer she would monitor, in that discreet way of hers, my reactions to his forced cheerfulness or, if he could bear it no longer, to his vast silences. With Mother's eyes on me I would watch Father observe the other patrons or stare out at the view, which was often of some unremarkable street or square, no doubt daydreaming or plotting his next move in the secret work I never once heard him talk about. At these moments it felt as if he were the boy obliged to pass a meal with adults, that he was the son and I the father.

After she passed away he and I came to resemble two flat-sharing bachelors kept together by circumstance or obligation. But then that tenderhearted sympathy, raw and sudden, would rise in him at the most unexpected moments, and he would plunge his face into my neck, sniff deeply and kiss, tickling me with his mustache. It would set us off laughing as though everything were all right.

CHAPTER 3

It is true; I did see Mona first.

She was sitting on the ceramic tiles that surrounded the rectangular swimming pool of the Magda Marina, looking at the underside of her foot. The tiles were decorated in a pattern that many years later, on a trip to Granada, I learned was a factory copy of a wall mosaic at the Alhambra. When I saw the original I ran my fingertips over the mosaic and let my mind return to that distant summer's day of 1971 in Alexandria, when I was twelve. Her hair was tied sensibly in a ponytail, and she had on an outrageously bright yellow swimsuit that made her skin seem darker, her age younger. For a moment, I thought her a girl. For a moment, the yellow strap running across her back brought to mind the yellow hospital bracelet that had been bound round my mother's wrist. The light shimmered blue and weakly off the water and onto Mona's body.

"This bit of skin is Arab; this, from your English mother," I would later come to tease her.

She was pulling her ankle, arching her neck, the ridge of her spine pressing against the yellow strap. Thinking back on it now, I am envious of the confidence with which I had approached her, as if I were crossing the road to the aid of a turtle on its back. Such natural self-assuredness has since eluded me. Whereas Father managed to shake off that cloak of shyness over the years, mine only got heavier.

I sat cross-legged beside her on the tiles and, without asking permission, placed the complaining foot in my lap. I proceeded to inspect each toe. She did not resist. Then, embedded in the soft underside of one toe, I found it: a brown speck of a thorn fading into the pink flesh.

"Last week," I told her, turning her foot in order to gain a better angle, "the same thing happened to me. It drove me crazy the whole day until I couldn't stand it any longer, and just before going to bed I pulled it out."

I captured the thorn between two fingernails. She flinched, but I did not draw back.

"Just like that," I said and held it on the tip of my forefinger to show her. Our heads were so close now that I could feel a strand of her hair touch my temple.

"Thank you," she said in an angular Arabic.

I could see now that her shoulders had eased.

"What is your name?"

It was an English accent. I was sure.

She ran her hand down my cheek, then held my chin and gazed at me. She had inconstant eyes: brown, green and silver all at once.

"Nuri," I finally said, pulling away. "Nuri el-Alfi."

"Pleasure to meet you, Nuri el-Alfi," she said and smiled a smile I could not understand.

I walked back to where Father was sunbathing. Now he had his broad chest propped up on his elbows.

"Who is she?" he asked, his eyes on her.

I thought of running back to ask her name, but she stood up, slid two fingers beneath the bottom of the swimsuit and stretched the fabric around her buttocks. The pattern of the ceramic tiles was faintly imprinted on the underside of one thigh. She turned toward us. I wondered if she was looking at me or at Father, or at us both together. Then she went to sit at a table where a glass of lemonade had been waiting. Father reclined, his elbow red with pressure, and closed his eyes. Under a perfectly cropped mustache his lips stretched into a precise smile, knowing, ironic, as if he was satisfied at his own intelligence, at having figured out a riddle in half the time. She looked our way again, lit a cigarette, then pretended to be looking elsewhere. Finally she closed her eyes at the sun. I watched her without restraint. I wanted to wear her as you would a piece of clothing, to fold into her ribs, be a stone in her mouth. I made as if I were walking around the pool to watch her from all angles. Suddenly she opened her eyes, looked at me, unsurprised, unmoving. She came to the pool's edge, dipped one foot in the water, then the other and tiptoed away. I watched the trail of wet prints evaporate. The glass of lemonade was still there, patient and full. One of the sweating waiters dressed in black bow tie and waistcoat took it away. I regretted not beating him to it. How wonderful it would have been to drink something intended for her.

I found Father turned on his stomach, the wood slats of the sun lounger marked red across his back.

×　×　×

I did not see her for the rest of the morning. And before we sat at our table to lunch I noticed that Father, too, was scanning the dining hall. I looked up from my plate every time someone walked in and, having his back to the entrance, Father glanced at my face as if it were a mirror. At one point he turned around to see who had come in, and I felt I had misled him.

After lunch most retreated to their rooms to escape the sun. A few Europeans remained stretched outside the shade by the pool, their skin the color of orange peel. A breeze would occasionally ruffle the pages of the books and magazines on the floor beside them, but the bodies lay shiny and still in the white heat.

I took my ball to the tended lawns that snaked around the rooms. Each room was constructed in the shape of a box with the front façade in glass sliding doors, mirrored for privacy. The structures hummed with their own air-conditioning, which on the outside hissed and blew hot. I felt spied upon by the guests in each room, even though I suspected they were probably dozing like Father. He would lie in the curtained coolness, one ankle resting on the other, the newspaper crackling between his hands, as he leaned slightly toward the lamp shade.

One room had its door open the width of two fingers. I could hear running water, an English song and along with it a woman's voice. I drew the door wide enough to enter but waited until my eyes adjusted to the shade. The room was an exact replica of ours, the same bedcovers, the same wallpaper and furniture, except that it had one bed that was as large as our two single beds combined. The bathroom door had also been left ajar, the yellow swimsuit hanging from the handle. I realized then that I had been searching for her, hoping to encounter her away from my father's gaze. I felt a feverish excitement at being in her room, inside the private chamber of this mysterious woman who was traveling alone. Who was she? How did she come to speak our language? So very few non-Arabs speak Arabic that when you encounter one it is as thrilling as spotting a friend in the audience of a vast theater just before the lights go down. And the way she moved, the way she looked at me across the pool, expressed a confidence of purpose that suggested she was not on holiday, that she had not come to just hang around, and so she immediately acquired the allure of those who, like my father, seemed to live their lives in secret.

I sat at the foot of the bed, placing the ball beside me. There was a pair of shoes in front of the armchair. One shoe lay on its side, revealing the pressed and molded cream leather of the interior. On the chiffonier there was a pearl necklace, a perfume bottle and a hairbrush. With my hand on the bathroom door handle, resting on the damp swimsuit, I looked with one eye through the narrow opening. I saw her naked body fogged by the shower curtain: the triangle of black hair blurred and moving like one of those blots that appear after looking directly into the sun. I made no sound and was certain she could not see me, but suddenly she said, "Who's there?" I ran, not caring what noise I made now, as fast as I could out of the room, remembering my ball only when it was too late to return for it.

x   x   x

As soon as Father rose from his nap, I told him.

"My ball wandered inside one of the rooms and I didn't feel it was right to get it."

"So?" he said, shaving. He usually shaved early evening, before dinner, and not in the mornings like most men.

"I just don't want anyone to think I was spying or anything."

"But I've always known you were a little spy," he said, smiling through the mirror.

He brought the blade to his neck and shaved off a strip of foam in one easy stroke.

× × ×

In the evening I found her standing in a black dress by our table in the dining hall, talking to Father, one hand on the backrest of the opposite chair, my chair. The pearls were encircling her neck. Her brushed hair fell heavily and knew exactly where, just above the jawbones, to curve back. And as I came close I caught the fragrance of her perfume.

"Here is your little friend," Father said in English when I was close enough to hear.

She held out a hand. I shook it, unable to look her in the eye.

"Speak, don't be shy," Father said into the awkward silence. "He attends English school," he told her.

Another chair was brought, another place set, and we dined together. She did not mention a word about that afternoon, but when Father went to answer a telephone call she smiled.

"Earlier there was a mouse in my room. A very large mouse."

And, again, with that feathery clasp, she took hold of my chin.

"Tomorrow come fetch your ball."

She sipped some water, dabbed the corners of her lips with the white napkin.

"Your father tells me you are twelve. For some reason I thought you were older."

She was no longer speaking in Arabic now and so lacked the vulnerability I had first detected by the pool. And because it was Father who had chosen to speak in English when I approached the table, I saw him as the one behind this transformation.

CHAPTER 4

The following morning I did not attend breakfast. I walked past the main hotel building, where the restaurant was, and on to the grassy paths that meandered around the rooms. The sea was quiet. I could just about catch the broken chatter and laughter of Europeans breakfasting in the dining hall. I pictured Father sitting there alone, reading the paper. I felt guilty. Then that turned immediately to jealousy, because the next picture my mind drew had Mona sitting opposite him.

I sat against the prickly bark of a date palm. The shadow of its crown spread around me and moved in the wind. I had her room in view. Were she to leave or enter I would see her. I then began to cry with a pain new and confusing. One of the gardeners in blue overalls noticed. The wide rim of his canvas hat rose and fell as he ran over. I thought of getting up and going, but the crying only became stronger. He bent over. "Malish, malish," he said, patting my shoulder. He never asked the reason behind my tears. My mind has often returned to this act of kindness. I remember laughing with him, but not about what. I remember his weathered face, his heavy eyes, unshaven cheeks, yellowed teeth, the smell of moist earth, but I cannot recall what had set him off laughing so infectiously.

I went to wash my face in the sea. A couple of dressed women, probably servants, stood waist deep in the water. Balloons of black fabric surrounded them and glistened whenever one of them moved. Their conversation turned to whispers when they saw me, whispers barely louder than the ripples lapping at my feet. I wished Naima had come with us. She had been our maid since before I was born. At that moment I felt she knew me better than anyone in the entire world.

A man in shorts and a baseball cap—in retrospect, he was probably a retired diplomat—with a tuft of gray hair at the center of his bronzed chest, jogged briskly along the shore.

"Morning," he shouted in English although it was nearly noon and we were both Arab.

I felt like going after him, shouting, "Morning morning morning," making stupid faces. Instead, I licked the salt off my lips and wandered back into the gardens of the Magda Marina.

Although I did not see a shadow appear beside me or hear her approach, I did not flinch when she sneaked from behind and threaded an arm through mine. Her lips were smiling. Her cheeks glowed with mischief.

"I have been looking for you," she said, and I felt the lump in my throat dissolve.

She walked ahead, leading the way to her room. As she moved, the wind moved and caused the slack gray cotton of her dress to hold for a moment the curve of her calf, the strong tremor of her thigh, the arc of a buttock.

"Stay here," she said and went into her room.

I caught my reflection in the mirrored glass: eyes red, cheeks puffy.

She came back and handed me my ball.

"Next time, knock."

I nodded and went to leave.

"No, silly, come back," she said, laughing, and drew the door wide.

I stood unsure of what was expected. Then she pointed to the armchair. I sat there, inhaling her smells, remembering Mother's wardrobe and how it smelled once I was inside it and the doors were pulled shut. But now everything was spilling out of the open door. I thought of asking her to close it, but it was a hot day.

The same pearl necklace lay curled in a figure 8 on the

coffee table. I imagined her coming in every night after dinner and not descending into this armchair but sitting at its edge, wondering what to do next.

"Would you like some juice?" she said, opening an identical minibar to the one we had in our room. "Guava?"

She placed the small bottle in front of me but did not unscrew the top, and I did not think it polite to do so.

She sat on the end of the bed, where I had sat the day before listening to her sing under the shower. I noticed a small cassette player on the bedside table.

"Do you like music?"

When I did not answer she pressed a button on the player, and an English song, fast and silly, filled the room.

She extended her hands to me then pulled me up. I pretended to be looking at the room. She closed her eyes and raised her arms above her head. With every move her breasts trembled a little beneath the gray cotton.

× × ×

I spent every minute I could with Mona. Whenever I had to leave her to go to the toilet my heart raced until I returned. And at night, when I had to go to bed, the longing and the excitement about seeing her the following day kept me awake. We swam in the sea, built sand castles and shared our bewilderment at the guests who would not venture beyond the swimming pool. We danced in her room to English pop songs that suddenly took on hidden depths to my boyish mind. My eyes were no longer downcast; indeed,

I often lost control of them altogether and would gaze without restraint at a particular part of her anatomy. Once, when she was looking at the sea, I studied her neck, a place where the skin was so delicate you could see the emerald veins weave their complex network. I kissed her there. She looked at me. Then, not so much out of shyness but horror, I looked away.

She told me about London, the city where she lived, about her mother, what she remembered of her dead father, "Monir." First name only, without a prefix, as if he were a friend or a lover. He had died when Mona was ten. He was a native of Alexandria. This was why she had decided to finally visit the city. Looking back now, I realize it must have been that early loss that had partly attracted Mona to my father, an Arab man fifteen years her senior.

"Monir," I said, as if in agreement. "He must have been the one who named you."

"I suppose."

I told her about my mother, how I, too, had lost a parent at ten.

She looked at me, nodding. I sensed she doubted my story. After what seemed to be too long a silence, she said, "It must be hard, for your father."

She showed me a photograph of Monir: a young, solemn Egyptian face with an English haircut. His overtly careful dress—a stiff white collar, a slim necktie that looked as if it were cut from clay, black waistcoat and jacket—expressed an anxiety, a self-conscious attempt at being taken seriously.

Later, when I lived in London, I often wondered how it was for him, an Egyptian, living in the Britain of the 1940s and 1950s. The slightly flexed eyebrows, sunken cheeks and pencil-line mustache seemed to signal something about this life.

In contrast, the one of her mother was taken more recently, in color, and showed the face of a calmly resigned middle-aged Englishwoman: handsome, with delicately drooping shoulders and a strong neck, a woman in her own country.

Mona, too, was an only child. She said she liked it that way, and I immediately said that I did too. And for a moment I believed it. I did not tell her how often I had longed for a sibling, particularly a brother; I did not tell her how, when Mother was alive, I felt like the minor character tossed between the only two protagonists who truly mattered, and how, after Mother's death, with Father hardly ever uttering a mention of her, I longed to share my loss, the density of grief, with an ally, an equal. I did not tell her any of this, not because I did not know how to say it or because I did not feel I could confide in her but because, there and then, sitting beside her and within the strength of my adoration, I felt invincible.

CHAPTER 5

There was no doubt then who among us was closer to Mona. She and I saw Father only at mealtimes. He spent his time sunbathing, reading fat books: one on the Suez Crisis; another a biography of our late king, with a portrait of the monarch on the cover.

Whenever Father acquired a new book on our country, he would immediately finger the index pages.

"Who are you looking for?" I had once asked.

He shook his head and said, "No one."

But later I, too, searched the index. It felt like pure imitation. It was not until I encountered my father's name—Kamal Pasha el-Alfi—that I realized what I was looking for. Kamal Pasha, those books would say, had been one of the king's closest advisers and one of the few men who could walk into the royal office without an appointment. And whenever the young monarch was in one of his anxious moods—perhaps suspecting his end to be near—it was Kamal Pasha el-Alfi who was often called to ease his fears. In these books my father was also described as an aristocrat who after the revolution moved "gradually, but with radical effect," to the left. I read these things about my father before I could know what they meant. And if I came to him with my questions, he would smoothly deflect them:

"It was all so long ago."

I rarely persisted because I knew that he was being true to Mother's wishes.

"Don't transfer the weight of the past onto your son," she once told him.

"You can't live outside history," he argued. "We have nothing to be ashamed of. On the contrary."

After a long pause she responded, "Who said anything about shame? It's longing that I want to spare him. Longing and the burden of your hopes."

Another book he had with him at the Magda Marina, one with which he had hardly parted since Mother died, was Badr Shakir al-Sayyab's *Rain Song*. At that time I would read passages of Father's books or a newspaper article that I was certain he had read because I wanted to follow a trail he had taken. And most of the time I could see what interested him. But I still cannot understand what the man I took Father to be, a man so single-mindedly committed to never-uttered plans, a man who consulted only history and news and who seemed to apply his attention with efficient precision to his designs, saw in al-Sayyab's poetry. I could not imagine him, for example, in the world of a line such as "the sea stroked by the hand of nightfall." This was Mother's territory. Several times I felt the impulse to say, "It's too late now to pretend you understood her." But perhaps I had misread him. Perhaps he did find a small landing place on the verses of al-Sayyab. Perhaps he did understand her. Still, part of my heart never ceases to blame him for her death.

Only years later, after his disappearance, when I returned to the family home in Cairo, did I notice that beside Mother's name, "Ihsan," inscribed on the inside of the front cover, Mother had also written: "November 1958, Paris." The month, the year and the city of my birth.

× × ×

When Mona and I joined Father in the dining hall, he never read the paper or looked into the distance but talked, looking more at me than at her. You could tell, though, that everything he said was colored by the intention of impressing her. She would sit between us at the table that was meant for two. And for the first time since Mother's death I watched that sparkle return to Father's eyes as he retold old anecdotes from when he was "a proud servant of the king." Father spoke animatedly about how, in 1941 when he was twelve, he had met the king's legendary uncle: a general who had led Ottoman troops in the First World War and spoke seven languages. The national hero shook Father's hand with the might of a "stone grinder," and when a few days later the Pasha died in an attempted coup, Father walked in the front line of the funeral. The closeness of the events was dazzling, but then, when after a perfectly timed pause he added that both events had made him cry, he provoked a smile from Mona.

It surprised me to hear Father talk like this; he rarely mentioned public life.

After a silence that the newly acquainted must occasionally allow themselves, Father said, "Before flying back to London, you must come visit us in Cairo."

"Perhaps another time," she told him and blushed slightly.

"No," I said. "You must come now. I have so much to show you."

"You can't come all this way and not see the Nile, the museums, the Pyramids."

Father and I were forming a united front.

"Well," she said, tilting her head to one side.

"You can see all the way to the Pyramids from my room," I said.

For some reason this caused them both to laugh.

"I wish," she said, touching my hand. "But, darling, my ticket, I won't be able to change it."

Piling the last remaining grains of rice onto his fork, Father said, "I can take care of that."

A new shyness showed itself in her eyes.

"I will call my secretary to rebook it," he said and closed his lips on the loaded fork.

× × ×

The following morning I found neither of them in the dining hall.

"They have already taken breakfast," the waiter said, pouring the orange juice.

I ran out to look for them. I found them walking by the sea, not arm in arm, but their paces could not have been better matched. Neither of them reacted when they saw me approach. I walked next to her for a few paces, let them pass, then ran and, not finding room between them, this time I walked by his side. Their conversation, like their steps, rolled on regardless. Father was exercising one of his old theories on her.

"Caravaggio is more important than Michelangelo because he took more risks."

"When was Caravaggio? And Michelangelo? I see. How interesting."

But this was Father's purpose, of course: to intimidate and impress. And Mona was easy prey, for she had little real interest in art.

They sat facing the sea. Their hands were resting side by side on the dry sand, his little finger over her little finger. I tried to imagine friends doing that.

"I cannot believe you have never been to Paris," he told her.

"I know, I know," she said, blushing but not pulling her hand away.

"Criminal," he said.

She let out a laugh different from those I had heard her give before. This one was louder and had in it the hard edge of hunger.

"I was born in Paris," I said.

"I know, darling," she said, bringing a careless hand to my cheek, then letting it rest again on her chest, the forefinger reaching beneath the blouse.

"Nuri, go and get my diary," Father said. When I was a few paces away, he added, "And the cigarettes, please."

CHAPTER 6

Two years earlier, my mother had died.

I recall how, during the edgeless hours of the afternoon, I would use her hip for a pillow. I would listen to the steady rhythm of her breath, the turning pages of her book. If I fell asleep, the sound would become a lazy breeze rustling a tree, or a broom brushing the earth. I hold the memory of her collarbone. I used to reach for it the way a rock climber would a sturdy ledge. I recall also her hair, strands as thick as strings. I would stretch one across my forehead, on my tongue, and feel it tighten like a blade. None of this would distract her from her reading. I would watch the wide blossom of her eyes scanning the lines, those same eyes that grew keen whenever I caught her standing behind a thick curtain in a game of hide-and-seek or when I revealed to her a luminous butterfly I had captured. How quickly her cheeks would redden then. She would speak, a warm whisper, before laughter flexed her throat. I am now above the ground, surprised by the softness of her square jawbone when I rest my forehead on it. I look at the shape of her ear. She was as close as I ever came to having a sister.

And then there were those cruel, sudden gaps, the clearings where she stood alone, not knowing how to return. Those were the days when she was unreachable. How her eyes would then wilt, looking at me as if acknowledging someone she half knew. Sometimes at night I would wake up and find her there, studying my face. She would force a smile and depart, quietly closing the door behind her, as if I were not hers. Other times she would lie beside me, two heads sharing one pillow. Her hands, the pale thin fingers that never seemed to match her strength, would be frozen twigs. She would tuck them between my knees or, if I were lying on my back, slide them behind my lower back, the place that is still hers.

In her last year her silences grew deeper and more frequent. Some days she did not leave her room. When she called, she called only for her faithful maid, Naima, who would also refer to her as Mama.

"Of course, Mama."

"Straightaway, Mama."

Naima would often be sent to the pharmacy for aspirin, sleeping pills, painkillers.

So old and persistent did Mother's unhappiness seem

that I had never stopped to ask its true cause. Nothing is more acceptable than that which we are born into.

× × ×

I remember the last night.

It was late evening. Naima had already changed out of her house galabia and into the hard fabric of her black dress, a veil wrapped tightly round her head, revealing the delicate shape of her skull. And there was the familiar carrier bag slung on her wrist, containing one or two but never more than three pieces of fruit, the round forms pressing against the plastic.

At Mother's instruction, every evening Naima had to go to the large fruit bowl that sat at the center of the long dining table and take home those guavas, apricots or apples that had passed their prime. Naima resisted this and would often argue the fruit was still good. Her resistance baffled me because I knew that on her birthdays Naima's parents gifted her with only an apple or just a handful of mulberries.

She stood there now, silent and hesitant, at Mother's door. She brought her hand up but did not knock.

"When she wakes up," she whispered, "tell her I went home. See you tomorrow."

She must have detected I did not want her to go, because she stopped and asked, "Did you brush your teeth?"

Every time I looked up from the sink I saw her in the mirror, standing outside the bathroom, her hands held against her waist like a person in prayer.

I followed her to the door and stood barefoot on the cold marble. She studied her foggy reflection in the long, narrow glass window in the lift door and with nervous hands tucked away stray hairs. She never stopped dreading the long journey home. On the occasions when her parents allowed her to spend the night with us, Naima would carry out her tasks in the house with renewed enthusiasm, insisting that she dust the bookshelves again, clean the bathrooms one more time, all the while cracking jokes at which no one laughed. The silences that followed these jokes always turned her cheeks red.

"Go on now, you will catch a cold."

But I did not move until the lift arrived because, regardless of her words, I knew she welcomed my attachment. There was always that elusive thing about Naima that needed confirmation not so much of my attention as of my loyalty, as if she feared I might, one day, betray her.

I waited for Father and only once dared walk into Mother's room. She lay on her side and did not move when I touched her ear. I went to my room and stood on my desk chair facing a photograph Mother had recently taken of herself. She was the one who had had it framed and hung it there. Her eyes stared back unflinchingly, but her jawbones were slightly out of focus, as if she were emerging from a cloud. I liked it because her face was nearly life-size.

I did not know then why Mother looked better in photographs taken before I was born. I do not mean simply younger but altogether brighter, as if she had just stepped off a carousel: her hair settling, her eyes anticipating more joy. And in those photographs you could almost hear a kind of joyful music in the background. Then it all changes after I arrive. For a long time, before I knew the truth, I thought it was the physical assault of pregnancy that had claimed her cheery disposition. Occasionally it would reemerge, this happy outlook, awakened by an old memory, like when she told the story of Father slipping over and landing on his bottom on one of the steep alleyways in Geneva's Old Town.

"His back white with snow," she said, barely able to speak from laughing. "Calling my name as he nearly tripped up the Christmas shoppers."

Father's face changed, a solemn expression suggesting he might be taking offense, which of course made the whole thing funnier. "I nearly broke my neck," he finally said.

"Yes, but your father has always been an excellent navigator," she said, and they both exploded into laughter.

I do not recall ever being so happy.

× × ×

I woke up on Father repeating, "Savior, Savior," and the sound of his reaching, anxious steps.

I stood in the doorway of my bedroom, my eyes weak against the blazing chandelier in the hall. Other people were there, two men in white. They held the front door open as Father rushed toward them, Mother slack in his arms. Her long and disheveled hair trembled with every step he took.

One of her dangling feet seemed to swing more rapidly. I ran after him, down the stairs. I remembered him once daring me to a race down those stairs, saying that he could descend the three flights faster than it would take me to get down in the lift. When the lift landed on the ground floor he had pulled the door open, trying not to let his breathlessness show, his eyes sparkling with satisfaction. But now when he saw me running behind him, he stopped.

"Nuri."

His eyes were red. Mother lay silent in his arms, her eyelids hard as shells. I paused for a moment, and the two men in white overtook me.

"Nuri," he shouted, and the two men looked at me. The expressions on their faces are still a source of horror.

I climbed back up, pausing at every landing, looking down the well. Then I ran to our balcony, my hands holding the cold metal balustrade above my head. I watched him carry her to the ambulance. One of her breasts was almost out of the gray satin nightdress. When one of the men in white tried to take her, Father shook his head and shouted something. He laid her on the stretcher, straightened and covered her body, caught the fall of her hair, wrapped it like a belt round his fist and then tucked the bundle beneath her neck. A siren started up. Father ran back into the building, through the stiff figures of Am-Samir, the porter, and his sons. Early light was just breaking, and they, too, must have been startled out of sleep. Somehow they did not seem surprised, as if they expected such calamity to befall "the Arab family on the third floor." The Nile flowed by strong and indifferent. There was hardly a wind to make flutter the bamboo grasses that covered its banks. The leaves of the banana trees hung low, and the heads of the palms seemed as heavy as velvet.

I heard the door of the apartment slam shut.

"Where are they taking her?"

He kneeled before me so his face was level with mine.

"She needs to rest. For a while . . . in hospital," he said and stopped as if to stifle a cough.

"Why? We can take care of her here. Naima and I can take care of her. Why did you let them take her?"

"She will be back soon."

He smelled of cigarettes, of others. He looked like he had not slept at all. I followed him into their room. An astonishing solitude was lit when he flicked on the ceiling light. Her form was still stamped into the mattress. Father's side was undisturbed. The room had the air of a place that had witnessed a terrible confrontation, a battle lost.

CHAPTER 7

He spent most of the subsequent days at the hospital.
Father, who had never had to look after me, was now con-
tinually asking Naima whether his son had eaten or if it was
bedtime yet.

"Has he bathed? Make sure he brushes his teeth."

I was suddenly spoken of in the third person. I had become a series of tasks. I could tell that Father was irritated
by having to bear such domestic responsibility. And every
time I cried for the mother from whom I had never before
been separated, he looked at once fearful and impatient.

"Naima," he would call, louder than necessary.

I asked to be taken to the hospital.

"The doctors are doing everything they can. There is
nothing more any of us can do."

"Then why do you spend the whole day there?"

I watched his nervous eyes.

Two days later he took us to visit Mother. At a set of traffic lights a boy, possibly my age, although he looked younger due to his thinness, tapped on my window. Round his arm hung necklaces of jasmine. He was wearing a red patterned T-shirt that reminded me of one I used to wear.

Rigid with shyness, Naima asked, "Could we buy some? Madam loves jasmine."

Although Naima did not address him directly, the question was clearly intended for Father. She was often wary around him. She would usually send me to ask whether it was coffee or tea that he wanted, if he was expecting anyone for lunch, and if there was anything else he needed before she left.

Father rolled down his window, and the thick heat of the day spilled in. The boy ran to him. Father bought the whole bunch, his eyes lingering on the boy's T-shirt. He handed the jasmines back to Naima and rolled up his window. His eyes now were on the rearview mirror, trying to catch a last glimpse of the boy.

Naima mixed the necklaces in her lap.

"You will get them knotted doing that," I said and immediately regretted it as she looked nervously at the rearview mirror.

"Aren't those the clothes we gave Ibn Ali?" Father asked.

Relieved, Naima looked back. We watched the boy run through the cars and vanish.

"Yes, Pasha," she said. "It looks like the same T-shirt."

Ibn Ali was one of the orphanages Father occasionally visited, often taking Naima and me with him, to deliver food or clothes or make a donation. There was also Abd al-Muttalib and al-Sayeda Aisha and al-Ridha.

"Don't let it upset you," Naima told him. "No matter what you do, you can't stop them working."

"But so young," he said.

"Not much younger than I was," she said softly and after too long a delay.

× × ×

Naima gripped my hand tightly as we went deeper into the maze of fluorescent-lit corridors. The jasmines were slung neatly around her other arm. The odor of the hospital was so unforgiving that every so often she would bring the small cloud of white flowers to her nose. I tugged, and she let me do the same. Father was already a few meters ahead. With every step he took the leather heels of his shoes were striped by the fluorescent light.

We found Mother lying under a cold blue lamp. The bedcovers were folded beneath her arms, one wrist was encircled by a yellow plastic bracelet, and a bleep hammered the silence.

Naima placed the jasmines at the foot of the bed and covered her face.

"Did I not tell you . . ." Father said, pulling her out of the room.

I was alone with Mother. I wanted to pull out the flattened pillows, to puff them up. Her skin had turned ashen. Her eyes were shut with an outrageous finality, a moistness lingering where the eyelids met. I thought of touching her, and the impossibility of it frightened me. My mind returned to a distant memory. I was four or five. She was getting ready for a party. I was crouched beneath the chiffonier, beside her feet: black high heels, stockings a color that made her skin look powdered. A thin fluorescent line hovered above where the black suede of her shoe met the stockings. An optical illusion. I traced it, erasing and redrawing the fluorescent with my finger. Then she moved. I looked up, smiling, thinking I had tickled her, but she was only moving closer to the mirror in order to scrutinize the exactness of her lipstick line.

Father was right: there was nothing any of us could do here.

× × ×

A few days later Father came home from the hospital earlier than usual. He went straight to his room. I stood outside his door for a minute or two then knocked.

"Not now, Nuri," he said, his voice uneven.

After a few minutes I heard the sound of running water in his bathroom. I remembered what Mother used to tell him whenever she found him in a bad mood: "Take a cold shower. It's what the Prophet, peace and blessings be upon him, used to do whenever he received bad news." And I remembered Father shaking his head. But that was when he was in no need of God. When he got out of the shower he called for Naima.

"Shut the door behind you. Where is Nuri?"

"Ustaz Nuri is in his room," she said, even though she saw me standing outside the door and passed her fingers through my hair and forced a smile before walking in.

He began whispering. A few seconds later I heard her give a short scream. Had he placed a hand on her mouth?

For the rest of that day Naima's fingers trembled.

Her eyes filled with tears when I asked, "Are you all right? Are you ill? Shall I pour you a glass of cola?"

Every hour or so she would come to ask, "Has your father spoken to you yet?"

Father stayed in his room, talking on the telephone. By sunset he called me in.

"Sit down. Let me see your hand." After a few seconds he said my name, then the words: "Mama will not be coming home."

After another pause he spoke again.

"She will never be coming back."

I pulled my hand. I did not believe him. I insisted he take me to the hospital.

"She is no longer there."

He restrained me, carried me to my room and locked the door on us. On the outside Naima cried, begging to be let in. Father opened the door and with astonishing tenderness pulled her to his chest and kissed her head. He held me too and began muttering that from here on life was never going to be the same, that God had felled his only tree and shelter. I searched but could not find a tear in either eye. This should not have surprised me, for I had never seen Father cry.

CHAPTER 8

The following day seventy-five wooden chairs, the sort most commonly found in Egyptian cafés, with a profile of Nefertiti printed on the seat, arrived. The porter, Am-Samir, and his silent children carried two huge speakers up the stairs. They slid off their slippers at the door, their stiff bodies swaying momentarily beneath the weight, and placed them, each taller than Father, in the middle of the hall. The angle at which the speakers were left facing each other suggested a quarrel. Then the porter and his children carried each piece of furniture that was in the reception hall into the dining room. Capsized armchairs were placed over the dining table, and their cushions were stuffed beneath. I watched Am-Samir's dark, hard feet sink into the rug. Each toenail curved forward into the thick wool. Each joint was crowned with little gray stones of skin, and each heel was like the thick end of a club. At what point, I wondered, will his sons' feet look like this? Noticing me follow him, Am-Samir placed a heavy hand on my head and, after a second's hesitation, kneeled down and kissed my forehead. He looked at Father. And Father, choosing to give Am-Samir the approval he requested, said, "Thank you." With lowered heads the sons followed Am-Samir out.

Urgency and grief had rendered Father, Naima, and me nearly equal. We arranged the chairs together. And at one point Father asked Naima her opinion.

"Where shall we place the speakers?"

"By the entrance," she said, embarrassed, and when he hesitated, she pressed on. "But that is where they are always placed, Pasha."

"Perhaps in your district," he said.

The possibility of a smile brushed both their faces.

"But it's people's duty to attend, Pasha. It wasn't I who set the custom."

"Enough. Lift," he said, and together they carried the speakers to where she had suggested, placing one at either side of the entrance.

We arranged the seventy-five chairs against the walls in conspiratorial silence. When we were done we stood in the middle of the room, and I hoped there would be something else for us to do, but then Father disappeared into his room and Naima returned to the kitchen.

The front door was left open. The reception hall began to resemble a waiting room. Not knowing where to go, I sat on one of the rented chairs. I counted the chairs that now stood in a chain. The first time I came up with seventy-four. On the second attempt I had seventy-seven. Only the fourth or fifth time round did I get seventy-five. Then I saw our next-door neighbor walk out of the lift. He did a double take. The Quran was not playing yet, so he could have thought we were preparing for a party. But something about me must have suggested bad news. I went to Naima in the kitchen, and the man followed in behind me.

"Greetings, Ustaz Midhaat."

"What happened?"

"Madam passed away," Naima told him, and, just as she did, tears appeared in her eyes.

Ustaz Midhaat looked at me now with eyes as wide as coffee cups. I moved behind Naima.

A few minutes later he returned with his whole family. Father came out dressed in a white galabia. He only wore a galabia to bed and so he looked as if he had wandered out from a dream. He sat beside our neighbor, saying almost nothing, his cheeks covered in stubble. Naima served them unsweetened black coffee and asked me to pass around a plate of almonds. Then Father waved to me to come.

"The Quran, turn on the Quran," he whispered.

× × ×

By the afternoon more neighbors arrived, people we hardly knew, and by nightfall the place was packed with silent mourners. I had never seen our house so full yet so quiet.

46

Naima was joined by an army of servants, lent by neighbors, whom she managed with a new authority.

I took the lift up to the roof to escape. The city stretched in all directions. It hummed and clanked like an engine in the night. The streets coiling into knots here and there. Not even the Nile tempered it. If I could I would have erased it, wiped it clean. I have never before or since felt such a careless desire for violence. Then I could feel a presence behind me. Naima, even with her endless duties, had noticed my absence.

× × ×

In the morning my mother's three siblings, Aunt Souad, Aunt Salwa and Uncle Fadhil, arrived from our country. I had never met them before, but recognized them from photographs. My aunts kept remarking how brave I was, how unusually long my eyelashes were, and teased me about my Cairene accent, my dark skin. They said because I was darker than Father and Mother that I was really my great-grandfather's son, who was, by all accounts, nearly as dark as I am. They tickled my toes, hugged me when I laughed, dug their faces into my neck and inhaled deeply before kissing. At night they took turns lying beside me, telling stories in the dark that usually included a mention of the waterfalls or pomegranates or palm trees of our country. If in the night I went to get a drink of water, one of them would appear behind me, asking whether I was all right.

They sweetened my name to Abu el-Noor, calling it out

whenever they saw me daydreaming. Silence, solitude, the roof, the slightest hint of contemplation worried them. If I was in the bathroom for a little longer than usual, I would hear one of my aunts whisper, "Abu el-Noor, habibi, are you all right?"

Father let his beard grow. It surprised me how heavily streaked with gray it was; he was only thirty-nine and the hair on his head was completely black.

Once, Uncle Fadhil embraced him, speaking solemnly and with a hint of urgency. Father eventually began nodding in a resigned sort of way, his eyes still facing the ground.

Another time the door of his bedroom was ajar, and I saw him cornered by my two aunts.

"He is unusually aloof for a boy his age," Aunt Salwa was saying.

"Let us take him back. He will grow among his cousins," Aunt Souad added.

"We will bring him up as our own," Aunt Salwa said. "This way, when the country comes back to us, he could play a role."

After a long pause Father spoke.

"I could not do that to Naima. She would never forgive me."

CHAPTER 9

Long ago, when Naima was ill with bilharzia, Father, under Mother's insistence, brought me to visit her. It took about an hour to reach the narrow maze of her neighborhood by car. But, as our driver, Abdu, was keen to tell Father, the journey on public transport took at least one and a half hours.

"Three hours round-trip, Pasha."

Father did not react.

Every time Abdu rolled down his window to ask for directions, the pedestrian would lean down and look at each of our faces. Eventually we found her street. It was so narrow that the car could barely fit through.

"Careful," Father would say in a near whisper while holding on to the handle above his window.

"Don't worry, Pasha," Abdu would reply, also in a whisper.

Raw sewage meandered down the middle of the road, passing neatly between the wheels. Father asked Abdu to roll up his window, but by then the stench had already entered the car. Above us clotheslines sagged under the weight and veiled most of the sky. Every so often Abdu had to press the horn, which sounded like an explosion in the narrow street. People then had to find a doorway to stand in, and even then we had to pass ever so slowly, brushing against their bodies. I watched a buckle, the detail of fabric, the occasional child's face. These people who lined the road stood still and kept their arms by their sides. I was sure from that angle they could see my bare knees on the beige leather upholstery.

Naima, her seven siblings and her parents all lived in a two-bedroom apartment in a building on the corner of that street. The side of the four-story building was covered in flaking red paint with the words "Coca-Cola" repeated across it. Abdu waited with the car. Children preceded Father and me up the stairs, calling out our arrival and occasionally stopping to look back, giggle, elbow one another before running up again. On each landing small plastic bags sat bulging with rubbish, many of them punctured and torn. Flies the size of bees weaved lazily around them.

"Don't touch," Father said, and I immediately pulled my hand off the railing. I placed it in his open palm. He did not let go until we were at the door of the apartment.

Naima's father, who was a security guard at one of the museums, met us on the landing in his uniform. He looked worried. The mother cried when she saw Father, then was ordered by the husband to go and make tea. There was hardly any furniture in the living room. One carpet, the size of a prayer rug, lay in the center of the tiled floor as if concealing an imperfection or some secret passage. Naima lay on a mattress in the corner. I sat beside her. She took hold of my hand. My skin burned in her grip. She neither smiled nor cried, but stared at me with a peculiar gentleness, as if I were a kind of nourishment.

"Nothing, really," the father said. "Her mother spoils her. She's just after attention. Aren't you?" he asked loudly toward Naima.

She did not respond.

"She will be up in no time," he told Father, anxiety blinking his eyes.

"She should take as long as she needs," Father told him. "We only came to wish her well."

The mother returned with a plate and placed it on the rug: crumbled feta and sliced tomato submerged in the pee-yellow of cotton oil. She stopped for a moment and looked at Naima and me.

"Isn't that right, um-Naima?" the father said. "You spoil your daughter."

She waited a few seconds before speaking.

"She loves him like a son," she said toward Father.

"Yes," he told her.

Although Naima would not let her eyes leave my face, she had taken note of this exchange. I squeezed her hand. I thought of saying something. Instead, I placed my palm on her cheek. She held it there. I thought perhaps the relative coolness of my skin was a comfort to her. But then tears welled in her eyes.

"Come, girl, don't be afraid," her father said, fear detectable in his voice.

And just as suddenly Naima's tears vanished.

The parents insisted we eat. Father shook his head. I wished he had been better able to conceal the frown on his face. Naima's father handed us loaves of bread. Mine was hard and speckled with flour-stones. The mother poured a thick black liquid, and when I asked what it was, the father said, "Tea, of course," and I was convinced I had offended him. About two centimeters of the powdered leaf sat in the base of the glass. Father kneeled down, broke a small piece off his loaf and dipped it in the solitary dish on the floor.

"There, thanks very much."

I bowed all the way down, feeling the blood gather in my head, and kissed Naima's hot forehead.

CHAPTER 10

Uncle Fadhil seemed to have come mainly to accompany the women. Being a man, for him the risk of retaliation for visiting his "backward, traitor" relatives was greatest. He was oddly awkward and mostly sat smoking. Whenever I sat next to him he would squeeze my skinny upper arms and say, "Flex."

Three days after they arrived, he told my aunts it was time to go. "Just in case the authorities think we are enjoying ourselves," he said, weariness curling his eyebrows.

Naima and I stood watching Am-Samir and his eldest son, Gamaal, fasten the luggage on the roof rack. We waved when the car pulled off, then went back upstairs. When I was in my room, surrounded by the smell of my aunts, I wept.

Our apartment struggled to resume its original character. Naima moved soundlessly, cleaning the indifferent surfaces, preparing our joyless meals. I felt a tremor whenever I heard the clang of pots in Mother's kitchen. Father seemed awkward and nervous around me. The beard was gone, and now he spent most of his time out or in his room. Naima no longer slept at her home but on the floor in my bedroom. There was an abstract urgency in the air.

The arrival of Hydar and Taleb, Father's old friends from Paris, rescued us. Hydar brought his wife, Nafisa, who spoke a little louder every time she addressed me.

Father gave up his room to Hydar and Nafisa. When they resisted, he said, "Listen, ask Nuri, I hardly sleep there. I prefer the couch. Honestly."

Then he insisted Taleb take my bed.

"This man knew you before you were born."

Taleb blushed, nodding.

I slept on the floor, in Naima's place, and she returned to the kitchen floor, where for a while, when she was young, she used to sleep in the winter when the sky got dark early and Mother worried about her on the long commute home.

Father relished his new freedom. Mother had not liked having guests, particularly those two, and this had been a recurring source of disagreement between my parents. But now he and his friends could stay up drinking whisky until the early hours. I would hear Taleb getting into bed. I think if he had not tried so hard to be quiet he might have made less noise. His breath would quickly fill the room with the chemical smell of alcohol.

× × ×

I could not help but feel that Mother's coldness toward Father's old Parisian friends was somehow part of the general unease that marked my parents' relationship to Paris. They almost never talked about their time in that city. And on the rare occasion that Mother did speak about how I came to be born there, she would always begin by telling me how Naima came to work for the family. I did not then understand how this detail mattered at all to the story.

She told me how she and Father had gone to Cairo expressly to employ a maid. And how, on the two-day drive back to our country, thirteen-year-old Naima hardly stopped crying. But every time they tried to turn back, she would object.

"At one point she began begging, so we continued."

Perhaps mistaking my silence for disapproval at the maid's young age, Mother said, "I wanted someone young, to get used to our ways, to be like a daughter," then she stopped, looked at her fingers, and only when she glanced up again did I realize that tears had been gathering in her eyes.

Eighteen months after my parents employed Naima, our king was dragged to the courtyard of the palace and shot in the head. Father was a government minister by this stage and, instead of risking ill treatment, detention or even death, he decided to flee to France. Naima was the last to step onto the boat, right behind my parents, pulled on board by Abdu the driver. They all stood watching the coast drift away, the smoke rise.

When the boat arrived at Marseilles, Taleb was standing at the dock waiting for them. Was he smiling, was he sucking at the end of a cigarette, did he wave? Mother did not like to talk about Taleb.

"Why? Is he a bad person?"

"No, not at all."

It never seemed like anger that she felt toward him. More like shame. And I think she thought of Paris and the time in Paris in the same way. So I was eager to ask Taleb, to find out what had happened after they arrived.

"Poor Naima could hardly stand," he said. "She had been throwing up the whole way. But your mother was determined. She didn't want to stay in Marseilles. I never understood that. She didn't even want to rest the night. She insisted we go directly to the train station and get on the first train for Paris."

I pictured her marching ahead and imagined Father behind her, glad for her stubbornness, glad that someone at least knew what to do next.

"And how was she on the train?"

"Who? Your mother? Like the Sphinx. I cracked jokes, but they were obviously bad ones."

"And Naima and Abdu? Did they go back to Egypt?"

Here Taleb looked at me as if I were suddenly standing a long way away. He seemed to consider the distance and whether it was a good idea to cross it.

"Abdu went back from time to time, but Naima didn't, of course."

"Where did they stay?"

"In Paris."

He seemed to have lost interest in the conversation. I thought of how to bring him back.

"Uncle Taleb?"

"Yes."

"How long have you lived in Paris?"

"Since university. Too long."

"Do you like it?"

"What does it matter? It seems to like me."

"Did Mama and Baba stay with you?"

"No, I found them an apartment in the Marais. Not ideal, but close to the hospital. A nice place, but a big step down from what they were used to."

"Not a hotel?"

"Six months is too long for a hotel. And in the end they stayed a year."

"Really?" I said. "I always thought they were there only a couple of months."

"You breathed Parisian air for the first eight months of your life. You will be ruined forever."

I liked Taleb. Unlike Nafisa's, his sympathy was not patronizing. He took me to places I had never been. Once, as I followed him through the arches of Ibn Tulun Mosque, I asked him, "Uncle Taleb?"

"Yes."

"What did my mother die of?"

He stopped and looked at me in that same way again but said nothing.

× × ×

Late one night, he on the bed, I on the floor, the room as black as a well and filling up with the smell of whisky, Taleb suddenly spoke.

"Sometimes it's better not to know," he said.

My heart jumped, but I attributed that partly to the fact that his words had snatched me from sleep.

"Some things are hard to swallow."

I recalled a dog in our street that had choked on a chicken bone. It wheezed and coughed and then eventually lay on its side and surrendered, blinking at me.

"You must know, regardless of anything, of her great humanity," he said, the word utterly new to me. I repeated it in my mind—humanity, humanity—so that I could later look it up. "She never ceased to be tender with Naima, who was innocent, of course. Ultimately, everyone is innocent, including your father."

After a long silence, just when I suspected he had fallen asleep, Taleb spoke again.

"You have no idea what he was back home. It's difficult, looking at him now, to believe he is the same person and

58

that the world is the same world. And he wanted someone to inherit it all."

My eyes peered violently into the dark. I recalled sitting with my parents at some station high up in the snowy Alps. I was behind them, their backs black against the white abyss of the valley. The wind was a mountainous wind. It would stop, then blow again, and Mother's scarf marked it. When they spoke they spoke in whispers.

"It's what you have always wanted," she said.

A long silence passed. Their heads followed a paraglider. Then Father turned with a hand pointing to the paraglider. When he saw my eyes on the target, he leaned back in the deck chair, the canvas sculpting his shape.

"What option did I have?" she said.

He did not respond.

× × ×

The following day Taleb, Hydar and Nafisa flew back to Paris. And although Naima changed the bedsheets, I could still smell Taleb's head on my pillow. I asked Naima to replace it.

"Why?" she said and pressed the pillow against her face. "It's perfectly clean."

CHAPTER 11

It was a relief when school started. Father seemed to relax. He returned to talking at the dining table. He even began to speak about what we might do the following summer. But when summer break arrived, he fell completely quiet about that. I did not mind; it seemed odd anyway that we should go traveling without Mother.

"It's not good for a boy to be home all day," I heard Naima tell him one morning.

That same afternoon he asked me to pack some beach clothes. "We are going to Alexandria."

Abdu drove us the following morning, and although Alexandria was only three hours away, for some reason Father insisted that we set off at six in the morning.

The Magda Marina seemed dull and depressing in comparison to the places Mother used to take us. I could not wait for the two weeks to end and to return to Cairo.

I could not have felt more differently the following summer, the summer we met Mona, when I prayed each day would last forever.

She was twenty-six, Father forty-one and I twelve: fifteen years separated them, and fourteen separated her from me. He scarcely had any more right to her than I did. And the fact that Mother was also twenty-six when she and Father married did not escape me. It was as if Father was trying to turn back the clock.

In the early autumn of that year, after our first summer with Mona, he ordered Naima to pack up Mother's things. And when she did not immediately comply, he repeated his order, using the same words spoken in the same tone, which was both gentle yet not to be questioned. As soon as she began, a new quality of silence descended on the room. He stood by, pretending to be looking through some loose sheets of paper. I watched helplessly as the sealed cardboard boxes began to mount in the hall.

"What are you going to do with them?" I asked.

He did not respond.

"You can't take them out of here," I said.

He looked at me and I knew that, if I were to take my eyes off his, Mother's things would disappear to some storeroom in the apartment block.

A couple of days later he ordered a carpenter to construct

a wardrobe across one end of his study. Mother's things were unpacked and put there.

He then flew to London, where he and Mona got married. I did not attend the civil ceremony, which Father had assured me was going to be "a quiet affair attended only by Mona's mother and, maybe, a few of their relatives." School, of course, was the excuse why I could not come along. But later, when their photographs gradually replaced Mother's pictures, I discovered that also present on that day were Hydar, Nafisa and Taleb, and other Arab-looking people, probably exiles from our country, their wives and children standing beside them.

At first Father did not say anything when he saw me peering at the photographs. Then he came into my room.

"Those people you saw in the pictures: they were passing through London." Then he returned again. "And what is wrong with having a few friends attend a happy day?"

× × ×

I had gone with Abdu to collect them from Cairo International Airport. On the way Abdu stopped by a florist.

"Nuri Pasha, I think it would be very thoughtful if you got them flowers. Your father would appreciate that."

I thought of what excuse I could give. Then, to make up for the hesitation, bought a huge bouquet whose giant fan could barely fit in the boot. Abdu carried it behind me into the arrivals lounge. The smell of jasmines, orange lilies and roses competed for space. Then Mona and Father appeared.

Behind their linked bodies there were two men, each with a trolley high with luggage.

She moved in with us, in the Zamalek apartment Mother had picked for its intimate view of the Nile. During those first few days I almost forgot our time at the Magda Marina. Every morning Father took his car to some appointment or meeting and Abdu drove me to school. Mona, more comfortable in the world than Mother had ever been, spent most of her time at the Gezira Club, where she played polo and tennis and drank tea with people Father and I were never introduced to. She had that English quality of placing the people she knew in compartments, as if fearing they would contaminate one another. Before long she had formed a wide circle of friends. Eventually, it would become necessary to resent her.

× × ×

But then in November, under the excuse of celebrating my thirteenth birthday, we took a boat up the Nile to Luxor, and the fire was reignited. The same sad hunger, only darker and harder to bear.

The boat was moving soundlessly. I could see through the small window in my cabin the waters parting behind us, the discrete ripples running wide like pressed skin, gathering pace then collapsing gently against the soft grassy banks of the river. This was our first morning aboard the *Isis*, clamorous Cairo far behind now. The capital's fat river had withered to a provincial waterway. Its banks pressed close and so seemed more reticent somehow. We were traveling upstream, south into the continent. Already the skin of the boys who occasionally ran along with our speed—waving, sticking out tongues, revealing buttocks—was a shade darker, as dark as Naima's. Another four days and we would reach the pale waters of Luxor, where, the captain had told us when we boarded, the waters are so clear you can see right to the bottom of the ancient river. Will we see jewels and ruins and things down there? I had thought to ask. But from where I was standing on the narrow lacquered deck behind Mona and Father and their two giant suitcases, speaking seemed impossible.

That night I could not sleep. The fluid motion of the boat combined with the muffled happy voices from the cabin next door kept me awake most of the night. The newlyweds did not fall asleep until the water's surface had turned silver: giggling, shushing, then a breathless silence, then sudden laughter. At one point, delirious with exhaustion and jealousy, I thought, They mean to do this; they mean to torment me.

Now that we were farther south, the sun had become braver. I lay uncovered, unready for morning, which came thick with heat. My T-shirt and trunks were sticky against my skin, my jaw slack on the pillow, when Mona walked in without knocking. I held my eyes shut, but she was not convinced.

"I have tried everything. It's past nine and he still won't wake."

She walked into the bathroom, leaving the door open. Without needing to move I could see part of her thigh. I heard the sound of her pee pouring into water—closer to a small stream than a fountain—then the scrape of paper. She washed her hands, splashed her face, gasping against the cold water. She sat on the bed. I turned and faced the wood paneling, reading the lines and twirls of the grain. She placed a hand on my back.

CHAPTER 12

What I then took for adoration was Mona's fancy to be adored. I imagine she found the torment and slow discovery of a boy-admirer all at once entertaining, flattering and pathetic. I think this now as I recall what happened next.

The three of us were taking turns diving into the passing river, then hurrying to catch up with the steamer. The other two would cheer as the swimmer chased after the ladder. The pace of the boat was gentle, but our excitement feigned danger. Every time the swimmer grabbed hold of the first tread, the other two would clap. Mona put her thumb and index finger in her mouth and whistled loudly. I wished I could do that. And ever since I have looked up to people who can as a kind of elite. At one point Father lifted her in his arms and kissed her. We had caused a spectacle. Clothed passengers stood leaning on the rail, watching us. They clapped as we climbed up onto the deck. Children looked at me. It was a performance, and we knew it. Our strangeness urged us on to act more, and we relished the questions we imagined our appearances and accents, our tongues that switched comfortably from Arabic to English to French, provoked in others.

"Ça, c'était vraiment rafraîchissant," Father called out from the deck.

And knowing full well his purpose, I replied, "Ah oui, c'était superbe."

'يجب أن نتذكر دائما أن الحياة للأحياء، يابني.'

Father plonked himself down into a deck chair, his chest heaving with effort, and I watched the dark wood beneath him darken further still. The captain stood nearby, looking at him. Father often elicited such admiration in men. The two began talking in that way men do when silence is unbearable.

Mona and I went to our rooms. She walked ahead of me, water pearls clinging to the small of her back, and when we entered the narrow corridor lined with numbered doors, her skin seemed luminous and green, the color of polished jade, until my eyes adjusted to the electric light. This moment is precious, I thought; soon it will pass, and I will be obliged to sit with them as they sip their aperitifs—which they did every day before dinner.

"See you on deck," she said, unlocking her door, smiling.

What makes those lips glisten, I wondered, and why does her blood rush to them like that?

I entered my room with the intention of showering, but

67

when I realized I was out of shampoo I went to her. She was already under the shower. I remembered the excitement I had felt when I sneaked into her room that first time at the Magda Marina. How magical it was to find myself in the same situation again. I stood by the dressing table, looking at her bottles and jewelry. I held the necklace and one by one let drop the pearls into the cup of my hand. I brought them to my nose. Her scent made a place in my chest ache. I buried my face into the silk scarf and felt myself grow thirsty. These were the objects that held her. When I heard the water stop, my heart quickened and I thought, I must leave before she sees me. I returned the objects, each to its place. The pearls made the soft sound of dominoes falling.

"Darling," she said. "I never thought swimming in a river could be so much fun."

It was peculiar to be mistaken for my father. There was nothing confidential about what she had said, but the tone of it surprised me. How bottomless it seemed.

"I'll never forget how you looked," she went on. "Those fantastic dives. Your chest."

After a short silence in which I did not know whether to speak or escape, she appeared with just a towel wrapped round her waist. The sight of her bare breasts caused me to turn around.

"I need some shampoo."

"You don't have to face the wall; I am old enough to be your mother."

She was sitting on the foot of the bed, holding a hairbrush. Her breasts were paler than the rest of her and seemed to deepen the pink in her cheeks. She left the brush beside her and gave me her back.

"Brush my hair."

I stood on my knees on the bed.

When I started brushing, she said, "No, start from the bottom."

I combed in silence, and whenever the brush met a knot I took my time.

"It's not true," I said, and as if knowing what I meant she did not respond. "You are not old enough to be my mother. You were only fourteen when I was born."

And again she did not speak, but this time it was a protective and knowing silence, a silence like the screen a doctor pulls across before he comes to inspect you.

Then Father entered the room. He quickly shut the door behind him and stood for a moment watching us. I felt an itch burn my skin and dared not meet his eyes. I focused on her hair, brushing diligently, as if it were homework. Without a word he went into the bathroom and shut the door behind him. I thought of asking him to pass the shampoo; I thought this would explain why I was there. But I continued brushing. He turned on the shower. I studied her back, down where the towel held her, tightening and loosening with every breath. And although I had chased all the tangles out and the brush was passing smoothly now, she did not ask me to stop. When I heard Father turn off the water I handed her the brush and left.

Back in my room I placed my ear against the wall. I could not make out the words. Father was speaking in that distant, unyielding tone of his, a thick silence separating each sentence.

× × ×

For the rest of the trip, Father would address me only when Mona was present. Whenever we were alone, he would look into the distance or pick up a book. But a few months after we had returned to Cairo, as spring was setting in, he called me into his study.

"Close the door."

I sat down opposite him.

"What do you think of studying in England?"

I shrugged.

"You remember London?"

I said nothing.

"You liked London. You will like England. And by now your English is strong enough. Both Mona and I think it a very good idea."

I could not bear crying in front of him.

"Is that all?" I said, then cleared my throat so as to explain away the cracked voice.

And it was with such merciless efficiency that Father moved me out of the way. The decision had been made: he had already enrolled me in Daleswick, a boarding school in northern England, and there was nothing I could do about it. Apparently, Mona had chosen the school.

"One of the oldest, no? Kings studied there, right?" he said that evening over dinner, looking at Mona.

"It certainly is one of the best," she confirmed, her face hardening with that self-congratulatory somberness that overtakes the English whenever they hear praise for one of their institutions.

But I would not be fooled; I refused to be impressed.

"Mama," I said, the word seeming to catch Father unawares. "Mama always told me that you moved us to Cairo so I could grow up in an Arab country." But then, louder than intended, I added, "What happened to that?" and ran to my room, where I had to wait a long time, until they finished eating and the table was cleared, for Naima.

× × ×

The suitcase lay open on the floor. Naima sat cross-legged beside it. Every garment I handed her she folded in her lap, then pressed tenderly into place. She, like me, seemed sick with silence. Mona was the only one who spoke.

"Isn't this exciting? You will make lots of friends, people you will know for the rest of your life."

Then out of the blue she asked Naima to go and make tea. And when we were alone she held my wrist and asked me to look her in the eyes.

"Believe me, if it were up to me, I would prefer you to stay here. It's your father; he wants you to grow up quickly. But I know, from how bravely you are taking this, that you are not a boy anymore."

CHAPTER 13

A week before I was due to start at Daleswick, the three of us flew to London. My throat tightened as we approached Cairo Airport early in the morning. Why must all horrible things take place early in the morning? I wondered. They treated me then with the sort of focused tenderness you show a grieving person. I was not allowed to carry my bag, and if my eyes lingered on an article in a magazine, Father would ask me about it.

We stayed a couple of nights at Claridge's in London before heading to school. Knowing how much I liked room service, Father telephoned my room just as I was falling asleep the night we arrived and insisted I call and order a hot chocolate. We spent most of the time walking around the West End. Whenever the two of them went into a shop

I waited outside. We wandered around galleries and in and out of museums. We were at the National Gallery, standing in front of Turner's *Calais Pier*, when, in a rare expression of sympathy, Father mentioned Mother. Not being in the habit of stopping in front of a painting for longer than a few seconds, Mona was already in the next room. I was still taking in the picture—the frothing, unbrushed curls of the waves, the peopled and tilting ships, the pregnant sails, clouds gathering like vultures, the chill of the whole thing—when Father said, softly, almost absentmindedly, "Your mother would have liked this." Then he moved on to the next picture, another Turner. I was startled by what he said. Anger was sudden. If it were not for its surprising and perplexing speed, I might have been able to express it more nakedly. Where I had repeatedly failed, an old painting succeeded. It was as if my father was not really talking to me at all. It was so rare for him to talk about my mother in this way. I did not know what to say. I wanted to ask so many things about her, particularly about what she was like before I was born. And I felt a window had opened, that Father was unconsciously allowing me to glimpse a part of her, if only for a moment. I made as if I was moving along to the next painting and came beside him.

"Baba, Baba," I repeated until I heard him hum. "Why that picture?"

"She liked this painter." He bent toward the text. "Turner. She very much liked this Turner. I don't know what it was about him." Then he put his arm around me, smiling, signaling the start of a private recollection. "One time, when we were on a boat somewhere—"

"Where?"

I realized I had spoken louder than I should have, particularly in an art gallery where people, for reasons I have never understood, are silent as they would be at a funeral.

He looked about us. I wondered if I had upset him, if he would ever finish the story, if my keenness had caused another long silence to begin.

"Ischia," he finally whispered.

"It sounds like a sneeze," I said.

"It's an island. In Italy. The Tyrrhenian Sea was high. Rough waters. She began to shiver. 'Are you all right?' I asked. She nodded, still looking away from me, out of the window. Waves were crashing against the glass. Then I heard her whisper, 'How beautiful.' A strong heart, your mother had." He gave a small laugh then looked at me. "A strong heart."

× × ×

I do not remember now why they did not accompany me all the way to the new school, and many times since I have wondered whether it was because Father could not bear abandoning me there, that his strength stopped at seeing me off at St. Pancras station.

I stood inside the carriage door, the small window pushed down. I gripped tightly the twenty-pound note Father had just handed me for a cab.

74

"Your housemaster, Mr. Galebraith, will be waiting on the platform," he said, looking up. "But in case you don't find him, there will be a taxi rank outside."

"Don't worry," Mona told him. "Nuri is responsible."

Then came the loud whistle of the conductor.

Father tested me one last time, asking me to recite the school address.

The train jerked into motion, its long, sad weight yielding.

"Call as soon as you arrive," Father said again.

Mona waved energetically. He remained still, his face solemn. Then—they must have thought I could no longer see them—she looked at him and he looked away.

× × ×

Seeing me struggle off the train with the suitcase, Mr. Galebraith wandered over to me. He smiled when we shook hands. Forgetting that it was mainly an Arab custom, I started to employ my left hand, but it landed not on the hand I was shaking but on his arm, round the bristly sleeve of his tweed jacket.

"Your father asked that we call as soon as you arrived," he said, leading me to a telephone box.

"Yes, Mr. el-Alfi, he is here, safe and sound."

But Father wanted to hear my voice, or that was how Mr. Galebraith had put it: "He wants to hear your voice," he said, handing me the receiver, now warmed a little by his ear. I could smell his breath: a sharp metallic smell. It might have been the breath of the callers before him, but somehow it left me feeling that there was something cold and hard about Mr. Galebraith.

× × ×

Two weeks later, without warning, they turned up. The head porter came into maths class.

"El-Alfi, you have guests."

Everyone at Daleswick, even the students, called one another by their last name.

"Ooh," the boys cooed.

"Better bring your things," the head porter said.

I collected my books, blushing the whole time, feeling embarrassed that I was having "guests" so soon after arriving.

I found them standing beside the rented car. Mona opened her arms. Father shook my hand, but then pulled me into an awkward embrace, kissing my cheek with too much force.

I showed them around, took them to the house where I boarded and brought them all the way up to my room. Father stood in his coat between the two narrow beds that were placed on either side of the square window, his head nearly touching the sloping eaves. The floorboards seemed to creak more loudly beneath his polished leather shoes. His eyes landed on the alarm clock he had given me.

"Is this your bed?" he asked, then sank a hand into the mattress. The bedsprings sang horribly. "Very poor quality," he whispered to Mona.

"That's what these schools are like," she said defensively.

"But for the money?"

I pretended I had not heard this exchange. The room embarrassed me; you want the people you love to desire your places. But as she was following him out of the room, Mona looked back at me and winked. I moved quickly to the front and continued the tour. I told them about the rituals of the place, and it pleased me then whenever someone greeted me by my last name.

"Here are the showers. And this is where on the weekends I make breakfast."

"You learned how to cook?" Father asked.

"Yes, my roommate Alexei taught me how to make an omelette," I said, hoping we would not encounter Alexei, as he was the only person on earth to whom I had confided my feelings for Mona.

After I was done showing them around, I could not wait for them to leave. And when we sat for lunch in the musty atmosphere of a pub in a nearby village, I felt impatient for the meal to end. Having them there was nowhere, neither the home I longed for nor the school I dreaded.

When they were leaving I overheard her say, "See, didn't I tell you? He has already got used to it."

He nodded before she finished her sentence.

Only then did I realize I had shown too much enthusiasm for the place.

CHAPTER 14

I could tell Father missed me, that in the act of putting me in boarding school he had run against his own heart. But my longing, growing more severe by the day, focused chiefly on Mona. She occupied my thoughts entirely. Odd to think this now that my whole capacity for hope and longing is directed at my missing father. Is the heart always failing itself or by nature unfaithful?

I had to restrain myself from writing to her too often, especially because she rarely wrote back or responded with the speed and in the manner I had allowed myself to expect. Some people manage to escape the obligation a sincere letter places on them. Mona was one of those. And she never gave me reason to think she cherished my letters; she never mentioned them. Perhaps this was her wisdom, if wisdom is the word—another would be ruthlessness. She must have known that I would eventually give up. When she did write, she scribbled something on the back of one of the numerous postcards she collected from museum shops. What she wrote was always brisk and unconsidered—"With best wishes" or "Keep well"—but I tried to read deep meaning into these platitudes. She would often enclose the petal of a camellia or lotus or common Egyptian rose—the fragrance still detectable. I read these silent gestures as involuntary expressions of her desire. The incongruity between these pressed fragments and the hurriedly written postcards haunted me.

The letters I sent were endlessly edited and pondered over and almost always too long. I kept a copy of the final draft. As soon as I dropped the envelope in the school post-box, the copy became more valuable, as it was then a record of what she would soon hold in her hand. I would reread it, finding more excesses.

It was November. My fourteenth birthday was quickly approaching. I thought surely now I would receive a fitting reply to my letters. On the morning of the day, I looked at myself in the mirror and decided that I was taller than she was. I rushed to my pigeonhole and found it empty. I had been away from Cairo for nine weeks—sixty-one days exactly. The marks of the summer sandals had already vanished from around my feet. It was so cold that most mornings I had to wear one pair of socks over another, and still by the end of the day my toes would be balls of ice in my hands.

Had Mona and Father forgotten?

I hated everyone at Daleswick that morning. I had told no one, not even Alexei, that it was my birthday.

Before morning class I ran to the front desk.

"No, Mr. el-Alfi, no one called for you," the head porter said.

But then, before the clock struck ten, he opened the classroom door and told the teacher, "Excuse me, sir, but Mr. el-Alfi is wanted at the front desk."

And whom did I find standing in the hall, wrapped in a coat and scarf, but Father, smiling. I almost cried but then remembered what Mother had told me about how I must be careful with my sadness. I expected Mona to be outside standing on the gravel driveway with open arms. And when she was not there, I thought, Maybe in the car. But she was at home, in the third-floor apartment on Fairouz Street in Zamalek.

Father had managed to convince stubborn Mr. Galebraith to let me skip school on account of it being my birthday. Mona was right: he could convince anyone of anything. I was even permitted to skip the evening study hour, and so was exempt from handing in my prep the following day. I only had to be back by lights-out. It was wonderful to sit in the soft, warm leather upholstery all the way to London when I should have been sitting on that hard wooden chair facing the blackboard. When we drove away, I hoped that by some miracle I would never have to return to that cold place ever again. Father let me choose the music.

"I flew all the way from Geneva to spend the day with you," he suddenly said, and I wondered if he had detected my disappointment about Mona not being there.

We walked through Green Park. The shade was thick and private in among the trees. It was one of those English days suspended between the seasons: the air temperate yet alive to the coming winter. Occasionally you heard the distant moan of an engine making its way up Piccadilly. Otherwise, the city was unusually quiet. It started raining softly. After a few steps Father opened his umbrella and it covered us both. I wanted everything good in the world for him: every dream he had, all of his secret plans, to come true. I suddenly was glad that Mona was his. A strange contentment toward the order of things fell on me.

We reached South Molton Street. We passed Browns, which used to be Mother's favorite London shop. In its window I spotted a coat.

"Mona would like this," I told him, and Father gave a short hum.

I went into the shop, and he followed me.

It was a fur coat with an impressive collar. I could see her in it, her hair rolled up in that usual way, like an actress in one of the old films.

"You should get her this."

Father's eyes bulged when he inspected the price tag and in English said, "It's horrendously expensive."

I suspected this was for the benefit of the shop clerk who was hovering nearby.

"Extremely expensive," he repeated.

"Well, then," I said, also in English, sounding like the fourteen-year-old boy that I was, "you ought to buy it because Mama Mona is both horrendously as well as extremely beautiful."

I called her Mama Mona because I knew that would please him.

This made him laugh, and he took the coat to the cashier.

I wondered whether he would ever mention that it was I who had spotted the coat or if he would quote to her what I said. Watching the lady work the silken tissue paper round the dark fur, I decided he probably would not, because when people buy someone a gift they like them to think it was all their idea.

We ate at Mona's favorite restaurant, Clarisse's. I chose it because I knew she would have. She believed they made the best cheese fondue in London, although she had agreed with me when I said it was nowhere near as good as at the Café du Soleil, a restaurant in Switzerland that we both liked but had yet to go to together. I, of course, ordered the fondue. Father ordered a large steak that bled each time he dug his knife into its thick flesh.

At one point, when I was returning from the toilet, I watched him from across the restaurant. He seemed a wholly different man from that distance. All the confidence was gone. He was leaning on the table with his elbows, one leg rocking. When I took my place opposite him again, he looked at me for a while before he spoke.

"Do you usually do this?"

"What?"

"What you just did: do you usually leave your food and go to the toilet?"

"I don't know."

He leaned farther across the table and in a near whisper spoke quickly. "From now on, never do that. And don't frequent the same places. Don't make it easy for anyone to know your movements."

I watched his face: his eyes wide open, anxiety curling his lips. He looked like a child who had just seen a ghost.

"Understood?" he asked when I did not respond.

I nodded. "Understood."

"Good," he said. "Good."

After we finished our food I asked for ice cream, and he ordered black coffee. When it arrived he lit a cigarette, which kept smoking in my direction. He seemed to have reached some other place in his thoughts. Now, from this proximity, I could see what she saw in him. His elegant, tailored clothes, his perfectly manicured fingers, and that defiance in the eyes. A man who followed his own law. And I wanted to be him. I wanted to have believed in and indeed served a constitutional monarchy. I wanted to hate, with the same passion, what he used to call "that infantile impertinence that passes for a revolution," then suddenly to re-emerge, with all of my refinement intact, a Marxist, "because each age calls for its own solution." I, too, wanted secret meetings in Geneva, allies in Paris with whom I had watched history march and worked to change its course. Sitting there at Clarisse's, I wished I could come to him as a stranger.

"Looking forward to the holidays?" he asked.

I nodded because my mouth was full.

"We will meet in Montreux. You two will probably arrive before me. I might be one or two days. But then we could all set off to the mountains."

I had no interest in skiing. All I could think of was being alone with her.

"What do you think? Is the Montreux Palace the right place?"

It was not his habit to consult me about such things. The Montreux Palace was where we always stayed. What he was really asking was whether I thought Mona would like that hotel.

"Yes. I think Mona would like it very much."

He looked relieved. "I think she will. It's beautiful. I will telephone Hass to book the rooms."

Hass was Father's Swiss lawyer and old confidant, and, although he was based in Geneva, he was the one who often booked our holidays. Even back when Mother was alive, Hass's office handled such things.

"Perhaps we should stay there the whole week," he went on. "What do you think? Or would that be boring?"

"But I am off for nearly four weeks."

"I know," he said, then took a slow sip of coffee. "You will spend the rest of the time in Cairo. I will take her to Paris for a few days before joining you there."

This was what he had been avoiding, knowing it colored everything that had come before: I imagined him thinking about it in the car, in the shop and even walking through the park.

"She has never been. And it's about time she got to know Taleb and Hydar properly. You will have to return to Cairo because Naima misses you. I didn't tell you this before, but more than once I caught her crying."

× × ×

He dropped me off at the boardinghouse and gave me a package from Mona. I stood watching the car turn and accelerate up the hill and into the trees. I could follow his lights in the darkness even when the car was deep into the wood: the light flickering in and out like a dying fire.

I turned to go into the house, my head busy with all the arguments I had not had with him. I ripped open the package on the way up to my room. Pajamas made by Hasan al-Eskandarani, the Cairo tailor who made all of our pajamas and bedding and towels. I pictured her going to his shop and selecting the fabric, discussing the cut. But, then again, for all I knew she might have telephoned her order in at the last minute. It was just before lights-out and several boys were already queuing outside the toilets with toothbrushes in their hands, the paste spread on.

Alexei was in bed but full of questions.

"Is it true today is your birthday? How come you didn't tell me? Was that your father driving off? Where did he take you? Why didn't you introduce us?"

It was nearly 10:30 p.m., and I could hear Mr. Galebraith's heavy footsteps coming up the long corridor. I put on my old pajamas and quickly got into bed. I could not wait to start another letter to Mona, but then Mr. Galebraith put his head through the door and said what he said every night—"Good night, girls"—and switched off the light.

CHAPTER 15

That night I blamed the same God I had countless times thanked for her: You should have made us the same age. Then my thoughts turned to Mother, and I panicked because I could not remember where I had last put her photograph. Before Father remarried I used to keep her always in my pocket.

"What are you looking for?" Alexei whispered.

"Nothing. Go back to sleep."

But I could see him in the black light, sitting up. He did not lie down until I returned to my bed. I pulled the blanket over myself and turned my back to him. When the tears came I did not sniffle, but then a succession of deep breaths gave me away. He did not say anything. I was relieved and cried openly now until the hardness passed. Long into the silence he spoke.

"You know what is the best thing about turning fourteen?"

Alexei was one year older, and I was in no mood for advice.

"Wet dreams. I got my first last year. They are fantastic. I don't know if girls have them. I think they probably don't. You see the woman of your dreams, the woman you will marry one day. That's what my father told me, and it's true."

I could not sleep after that. And long after Alexei stopped talking, I had to wake him to borrow his pen-size flashlight, which he and I called the James Bond pen, so that I could write my letter from beneath the covers. I had to be careful because at this time Mr. Galebraith took his dog, Jackson, walking in the fields around the house.

I missed her so severely that I had to stop writing and shelter the hurt I felt for her in my chest. I shut my eyes and tried to see her eyes, hear her voice, smell that place on her neck that she said was mine and only mine. And that was how I slept.

× × ×

At 6:40 a.m. I lay fully dressed in my uniform but under the covers, having a second go at that letter. It seemed even colder now that it was morning. The blue sky, if it was there, was entirely sealed behind rough clouds. The trees were leafless and black. When she had come here with Father, two weeks after I started at Daleswick, she said how she loved the English countryside, how romantic she found winter, how much she missed England. And when I had said it was gloomy, she said it was exactly that gloominess that made it romantic and asked me to read *Wuthering Heights*. Now that I had read that book, I still could not understand what she meant. There were boys as old as eighteen at Daleswick; was that how long Father intended on keeping me here? I began by thanking her for the pajamas, and then I asked whether she knew about wet dreams and whether she, too, thought them fantastic. I asked whom she had seen in her dream, whether it was my father. Then I had to stop writing and rush to breakfast.

× × ×

Alexei's world was completely new to me. Even though he had a tendency to boast, when he talked I rarely wanted him to stop. I would lie on my bed, hands clasped behind my head, and watch him like you would a film.

"Papa is now in Hamburg."

"What is he doing in Hamburg?"

"He's principal conductor of the symphony orchestra," Alexei said proudly.

This conversation took place early in our acquaintance. I had just arrived at Daleswick. Alexei had been there a year already, but he still had a thick German accent.

"Before Hamburg we were in Jena, where he was conductor of the philharmonic, and before that we were in Stuttgart because he conducted the Stuttgart Radio Symphony Orchestra. He had been offered the job of principal conductor of the Vancouver Symphony Orchestra in Canada, but he did not want to disturb our education. Which is why my sister and I finally had to be sent to boarding school: Annalisa had to go somewhere near Düsseldorf, poor her."

"Do you miss Germany?"

"I miss Annalisa. She can be very annoying, but she's also really funny. She knows the names of most stars."

"Actors?"

"No, the ones that light up the sky. And I miss Papa too. In the mornings he would always be the one to wake us. If I was being lazy, he would scrape his chin against my face before shaving. And my mama, of course. I miss her very much. Mostly her singing." Then he looked at me with tearful eyes and said, "I don't know why I said that."

After a long pause, he added, "They named me Alexei after Alexeyevskaya, the Moscow Metro station where Papa first kissed Mama. He says his knees wobbled. She says she did not notice a wobble. They met in Moscow because Mama was also a musician there. She was a singer. But not anymore. And they named Annalisa after Annalisa Cima, Eugenio Montale's 'muse'—that means the person who made him write good poems. My parents love the poems of Montale. Have you ever read them?"

Some boys at Daleswick never stopped trying to go back. They would tell you about the lives they came from, the lives from which they were now excluded. But such boys were usually dull, did not know nearly as much about music and poetry as Alexei did. I almost called him my Alexei there, because, among the mild yet constant disdain of the English, this German boy and I had formed an alliance. We took pleasure in the knowledge that being Arab and German were equally disapproved of here, and that intensified our intimacy and the allegiance we felt toward each other. This is why we insisted on always calling each other by first name.

"Does your name have a meaning in your language?"

"It means my light. My father chose it."

"What does your father do?"

I never was quite sure how to answer this question. Back in Cairo, when I was asked, I used to say retired minister, because that was what my mother told me to say. For a long time I thought that was an actual job title. I knew that Father did not have a job; that he did not need to work for money; that he had inherited a good amount from his father, who was the last in a long line of silk merchants: there was a book on the shelf by the man who had started it all, Mustafa Pasha el-Alfi, chronicling his long and slow travels to China some six hundred years ago. And, of course, I assumed all fathers were like my own: the little time they spent at home they spent, like recovering warriors, resting, reading in their studies, before returning to the secret obsession to which they were devoted. And although he never spoke about it, I always had a vague notion of what my father's obsession might have been. Perhaps those silences when someone, usually a guest, mentioned the military dictatorship that ruled our country, or when a visiting relative would say things like, "The road you are traveling has only one end," were what told me, even as a young boy, that my father had committed himself to fighting a war.

"So?" Alexei persisted.

"He's also a conductor," I said.

"Really? What a coincidence! Which symphony? I knew we were brothers, I knew it. So which one?"

"I'm not sure."

"What do you mean, 'not sure'? How could you not be sure? It doesn't matter if it's a small orchestra, just tell me."

"I can't remember," I said and felt my face burn under his gaze.

"Or do you mean a bus conductor? Or maybe he's a conductor of traffic? Or an electrical conductor?"

He laughed, and I thought it best to laugh too.

CHAPTER 16

The day before I was due to fly out to Montreux for the Christmas holiday, Mr. Galebraith stuck his head round the door and said, "A lady named Mona is on the phone."

I shot past him, running down the stairs, taking three steps at a time, not stopping when he shouted, "Slow down!"

"I can't wait to see you, my sweet peanut," she said.

Longing was a stone in my mouth.

"I have just checked in. I love this hotel. I will see you at the airport," she said and hung up.

The two-hour flight to Geneva seemed to last forever. How impatient I was with the hands of the wristwatch.

Father was in Zurich, Bern or Geneva; it was never clear. Mona and I had at least one or two or maybe even three days alone ahead of us. That was all I cared about.

×　×　×

Her cold-blushed cheeks seemed the only color in the gray arrivals lounge. She was not wearing the fur coat. He must have not told her, I thought, that I was the one who picked it out. We sat facing the same way on the train to Montreux. Several times I secretly dug my fingers into my thighs.

When we arrived at the hotel I had to abandon my luggage with the bellboy by the entrance because Mona was pulling me toward the lift. As soon as the doors drew shut she wrapped her arm in mine, turning her fingers round the part between the elbow and the wrist. I watched our foggy reflection against the polished brass doors. I had been wrong: I was not yet as tall as she was, but nearly.

There was always lightness to the way Mona held me, as if she were not really there. My mother, on the other hand, would always hold my hand too tightly. Whenever I pointed it out she would apologize and loosen her grip, only to forget and return to squeezing my fingers again as if they were strands of a slippery rope.

I suggested to Mona that, until Father arrived, we should share their suite. She looked at me as if I had asked her to take off her clothes.

"To save money," I explained.

She laughed. "And since when have you worried about such things?" She kissed me below the jaw, then took me to my room. We both stood on the balcony that looked out onto the luminous blue lake. The surface was a mirror to the blue sky and the passing clouds. It turned the weak winter light a shade darker.

"Tonight," she said. "Let's dine at the Café du Soleil and stay there until they kick us out."

When the bellboy walked in with the bags, she let go of my hand and cleared her throat. As soon as he left she let out a wicked laugh.

× × ×

It shames me to admit that even the tragedy that followed did not corrupt the memory of those three days spent in Montreux alone with Mona. If anything, and perhaps exactly because of what happened next, it glimmers still in my mind with the vividness of a dark jewel.

We took long walks by the lake, excursions punctuated by stops at cafés for tea, cake and ice cream. I was always too willing to hold her coat as she slipped her bare arms into the black satin lining. She liked fur coats because they allowed her to continue wearing her favorite sleeveless fitted black blouses underneath.

"Where is your new coat?"

"I am saving it for when Kamal is here."

My twenty-seven-year-old stepmother looked younger than her years, and I, even then, gave an impression that I was older. Few of the fourteen years that separated us would have been clear to a stranger. Once, in a busy café, aware of the attention of those at the table beside us, I leaned across, found a deviant strand of hair and tucked it behind her ear. She pulled back. I tried to imagine the questions our intimacy provoked: did they think her a careless adulteress occupying herself with a young lover? And when we left I took pleasure, too, from the envious, congratulatory looks I received from boys my age who walked in small groups by the lake. A scrupulous observer would have, of course, noticed the awkward nervousness her beauty caused in me, but my deliberate and shameful self-delusion, which she always found a way to encourage, persisted. She slipped her arm through mine, marrying her shoulder to my back so I was slightly in front, like an officer leading the way. After a few paces she let go and drifted ahead, looking at the water, no doubt wondering why Father had not telephoned. Her hair moved slightly against the afternoon breeze.

On the way back we passed two lovers locked in a kiss, and although I did not think I was staring, she pinched me and said, "Stop, you are too young for such things." But then she insisted I try on a jacket and tie she spotted in a shop window near the hotel. When I put them on, she shook her head and said, "Too grown-up."

× × ×

Every time we returned to the hotel she would ask at the reception if anyone had called. And the answer was always no. Going up in the lift, she would take a long look at the ground or say, "I don't know why he hasn't called," or, "He never tells me where he is."

Father's delay was like a cloud that grew thicker with

each passing day. By the evening of the third day, even I wanted him to come or call. I was woken up that night by the stone-white light of a full moon. It held the room in its cold, harsh glare. My heart thundered. I called her room and let the telephone ring until she answered.

"Kamal?"

"No, it's me. He's not back?"

"No, darling, go to sleep. He'll be here tomorrow."

×　×　×

To restore her "fading French," Mona had vowed to read *La Tribune de Genève* every morning over breakfast. If not for this detail, we would not have learned, the following morning, of the "lovers separated by force in the night," for I was not then in the habit of reading newspapers.

CHAPTER 17

She let go of the newspaper, but only when I tugged.

"Oh God," she said.

For a moment the terrace we were sitting on seemed in danger of tipping over and chucking us into the dark lake. I looked up, and the paragliders were still there, suspended in mid-distance.

"Come on, we need to leave. Call the police. Why didn't we hear anything? Shit. Come on," she said. Then she stood up and leaned for a moment on the breakfast table.

She hurried off toward the lift. I followed her.

In the room she began to pack. Her movements were furious. Every so often she would wipe the tears then continue.

I tried to read the article. The difficulty was not only due to my poor French but because my eyes could hardly focus on the words. Each letter seemed powered by its own little engine.

"Today, in the early hours of the morning, the ex-minister and leading dissident Kamal Pasha el-Alfi was kidnapped from an apartment belonging to a Béatrice Benameur, a resident of Geneva."

The mademoiselle—or, who knows, madame—looked at least Father's age, which, because of his preference for younger women, made her seem older and somehow formidable. But the name struck me as disingenuous. As indeed did her expression of grief in the black-and-white photograph that was printed beneath the headline of "Un couple séparé de force au milieu de la nuit." I was irritated by this; no evidence was supplied that the "lovers separated by force in the night" were indeed lovers and not friends, colleagues, associates or even enemies. And these suspicions only hardened when I read that, along with his wristwatch, cigarettes and silver lighter, Father had apparently left his wedding ring on the bedside table. Father always slept with his wedding ring on. This was an important detail because, as far as I could see, these personal objects were the only evidence that he was ever in the room. Anyone could have stolen them or purchased replicas and planted them there in order to fabricate a kidnapping.

Mona was now nervously paging through the telephone book.

Perhaps, I thought, to elude his pursuers or escape some unwanted circumstance, Father himself might have orchestrated this vanishing act. He might need to send us a message or he might be on the way to the hotel as we packed.

"We mustn't leave yet," I said. "Not now; Father might come and not find us."

She looked at me and I felt the need to explain myself. But then a knock came. I ran to the door. It was the bellboy, handing me a small envelope. It contained a telephone message from the night before.

"Why was I not given this earlier?" Mona snapped.

"It arrived late, madame," the bellboy said.

I stood beside her, and we both read the note:

"Call me immediately—Charlie HASS , Geneva." It listed a telephone number.

Mona sat on the edge of the bed, the telephone on her lap. I sat beside her, desperate to hear every word. She let me; she did not move the receiver to the other ear. All that Father's lawyer told us was, "You must come as soon as possible."

× × ×

On the train to Geneva we hardly spoke. I looked out onto the silver day. A slim road appeared down below, a black snake vanishing in and out of the thick growth. Houses on the passing hills, smoke seeping through the chimneys. How could I have not expected it? I did expect it. Did I not know that he had powerful enemies, that he was often followed? Why else was he so careful, so secretive? What would they be doing to him? Will I ever see him look at me again?

All that I did not know about my father—his private life, his thoughts, why he was kidnapped and by whom, what he had actually done to provoke such actions, where he was at this moment, whether he could be counted among the living or the dead—was like a mask that suffocated me. I felt guilty too, as I continue to feel today, at having lost him, at not knowing how to find him or take his place. Every day I let my father down.

I could no longer bear the presence of the woman who now sat beside me, hiding her eyes behind dark glasses, the tip of her nose glistening red. I could not understand why Father had married her. I held my palm out, and she handed me the article again.

× × ×

The window behind Béatrice Benameur showed no morning, just two black rectangles separated by a thin white frame. Her eyes, delicate with sleep, fragile from the shock, peered out of the photograph. Her hair was flattened, and when I brought the newspaper close to my face I was able to see sleep marks on her cheek, the marks of folded fabric. The photographer must have arrived on the scene unusually quickly. And suddenly it became reasonable that, out of respect for his wife, Father had decided to take off his wedding ring before lying next to this Swiss woman. Or perhaps it was not respect at all but because he had been taking a bath or cooking a meal. Also, the name, Béatrice Benameur, which had sounded false, now seemed perfectly credible, and it was also perfectly credible that she should have been horrified on being awakened abruptly by balaclavaed men restraining the arms, taping the mouth of the hunted Arab lying beside her, his bare chest heaving, his place on the mattress remaining warm for a long time after they had taken him, her hand on it, and her eyes for many minutes disbelieving what had just taken place, the speed of it, hearing what he sometimes told her when she was impatient with their arrangement: "Everything can change in a blink of an eye, my love," a statement designed, no doubt, to kindle hope. Or at least that was how, sitting between Mona and the window on that train to Geneva, my mind imagined it. For all I knew he never called her "my love" and she never had expressed impatience toward their "arrangement." Then I saw him standing up and leaving, guided only by suggestion, a tilt of one of the balaclavaed heads. I imagined this even though the article stated that "there were visible signs of resistance," that "blood was found on the victim's pillow," and that "the lamp shade beside him was smashed."

CHAPTER 18

For some reason, I had imagined Monsieur Hass to be a short man with a round, bespectacled face. Instead, when the train pulled into the station at Geneva, Mona pointed out a tall, wiry figure standing on the platform.

"There he is."

I watched him from the window of the train carriage. He had not spotted us yet. His features hinted at austerity. He had a head of straight black hair that was fixed back with the use of some sort of wax. He kissed Mona's cheeks.

"I am so sorry," he said.

When he shook my hand, his eyes remained on me a second too long.

His suit was black, his raincoat was black, and his tie was a matte slate gray with tiny white dots.

"This way," he said, and we followed him.

He walked quickly, the split tail of his coat lifting. When we were inside his car, he spoke.

"I saw him the night before. Everything was all right."

"When did you hear?"

"The night it happened."

"Then why didn't you call?"

"I did."

"You called the following evening."

After a long pause, he said, "I was waiting for something good to report."

He booked a twin room at a three-star hotel, the sort of place where I could never imagine Father staying. After we checked in he drove us to the police station. A man behind the counter listened to Hass, then handed him a form to fill out. The inspector would contact us, Hass said.

"I will leave you to rest," he said when he dropped us off at the hotel.

Mona and I spent the rest of the afternoon in the hotel room, by the telephone. Around sunset Mona called the police station. She was handed from one official to the next until her French failed her. Then I tried, and the same thing happened. After a short while the telephone rang. It was Hass. Mona spoke to him so softly I could barely make out what she was saying.

"He will stop by first thing in the morning," she said.

By nightfall she and I pulled ourselves out of the room. We walked slowly, aimlessly and a few steps apart. We passed the Café du Soleil and neither of us said a word. Eventually we walked into a fast-food restaurant and sat down under the indifferent lighting and ate in silence.

× × ×

The following morning we walked behind Hass, who walked faster than anyone I had ever met, to the police station. We stood facing the same attendant. This time he nodded and pointed to the chairs lined against one wall. Mona and I sat down, but Hass stood in his long coat. The attendant whispered down the telephone, and after a few minutes another man, dressed in a suit, appeared through a door on the other side of the counter. He stood beside the attendant, looking through some pages. Mona was already making her way to the counter. The man extended his hand.

"Inspector Martin Durand," he said.

Hass then introduced himself as "the family lawyer."

The inspector unfastened an invisible latch and lifted up the counter. Mona, Hass and I passed through. He led us into a room that had nothing in it but a table and four chairs. He apologized for not seeing us sooner. He asked us to tell him what we knew. We told him we did not know anything, that we only knew what we had read in the paper.

"What were you doing in Switzerland?"

Mona spoke, he wrote and only occasionally did he look up from his pad. Whenever he asked a question his head would begin nodding even before Mona answered. Every time she mentioned a place he would repeat the name out loud: "Cairo," "Daleswick College," "Montreux Palace," until it began to seem as if these places were somehow guilty or at least partly to blame. Perhaps this was why Hass felt obliged to clarify:

"They are here on holiday."

"I see," the inspector said.

"Can we see the woman?" I asked.

He looked at me. "Which woman?"

"Béatrice Benameur."

Mona said nothing. Her eyes were on the edge of the table.

"Do you know Béatrice Benameur?"

The inspector's question was aimed at Mona, but she did not answer.

"Then I don't think that would be a good idea," he said toward Hass, whose face remained as still as a wall.

Suddenly, Mona began to object. Her voice rose in fury. But Durand silenced her with a move of his hand and firmly repeated, "It would not be a good idea."

Hass did not speak.

After a short silence the inspector spoke again.

"We are doing all we can in difficult circumstances. This is a complicated case, not helped by the fact that the journalist was on the scene before us, therefore compromising the evidence. But I assure you we are treating it as a priority. Now, if you would like to follow me to the front desk, you can collect your husband's personal items."

We were handed a small sealed plastic bag that contained Father's wristwatch, cigarettes, silver lighter and wedding ring.

"We found these on his bedside table," he said.

Mona looked at the inspector. I knew what she was thinking: Father's "bedside table" was not in Geneva, but with her in Cairo.

× × ×

Back at the hotel Mona sat at the edge of the bed with her small address book open beside her. She turned the pages slowly.

"Do you need the bathroom?" she said.

I waited until I heard the shower, then located Hass's number and dialed it.

"Why won't the police let us see Béatrice Benameur?"

"She doesn't know any more than what you know," he said. The silence that followed seemed to trouble him too. "She just happened to be there," he added.

A little while later, he called back. Mona answered.

She fell silent for a while, listening to him. I wondered what he was telling her.

"You spoke to her?" she said. "I see. And what did she say? . . . What, right now? OK, give me half an hour," she said, and hung up. "He's on his way."

"What did he tell you?"

"That she's willing to see us." Then, to herself, she repeated, " 'Willing to see us.' "

After a few seconds I could no longer stand the boom of her hair dryer. I waited in the lobby, occasionally going out onto the street, walking back and forth in front of the entrance to the hotel.

× × ×

In the car I watched the back of Monsieur Hass's head as he drove. I wondered what he knew, what he was thinking at that moment. The slicked-back black hair looked part of the effort to keep what he knew silent. There was something unrelenting about the strong neck too. And from this proximity I could detect the familiar musky fragrance of Father's aftershave cream. Mona sat beside him, facing ahead, her eyes hidden behind the sunglasses. Her neck, rigid and slim, seemed in danger of snapping.

"Have you met Béatrice Benameur?" I asked.

All I could see of Hass's face in the rearview mirror were his eyes, which he kept on the road. Separated from the rest of his face, they looked almost feminine.

"Yes," he said, a few seconds after turning in to a quieter, smaller street.

I expected Mona to react, but she said nothing.

I spotted the street name: Rue Monnier—strangely similar to Monir, Mona's father's name.

"Why was she there?" I asked.

He did not respond, and no one spoke until he parked and turned off the engine.

"Is this it?" Mona asked in a barely audible voice.

"Yes," he said.

Neither of them moved. Perhaps Hass was hoping Mona or I would change our mind, ask to be driven back to the hotel.

"Nuri, can you wait outside the car for a minute?" Mona said.

I stepped out of the car. Hass rolled up his window. I could hear absolutely nothing of what they said. A few anxious minutes later they emerged. We crossed the street to a building with an arched entrance flanked by plaster moldings of babies with bloated bellies. He pressed the buzzer, and it echoed loudly in the empty street.

"Is this where she lives?" Mona asked—which even she must have known was a pointless question.

Hass continued facing the door.

I felt all moisture leave my mouth. Standing in front of the building from where my father had been taken presented what seemed to be a real and rational danger of being kidnapped or shot in the back or crushed under a large object falling soundlessly from one of the windows. I wanted to say to both of them, "This is dangerous," or pull them back by their sleeves, but I remained fixed to my place, and only after I noticed Mona's eyes on me did I realize that I was shivering. She came close, her shoulder touching mine, and then I felt the burn of her hand on my back.

"I called. I don't know where she's gone," Hass said.

He pressed the buzzer again, and this time the street seemed to amplify the horrible ring even more loudly. No sound came from inside the building. Mona's breath changed; I thought she was about to say something, but she just stared intently at the door in front of us.

CHAPTER 19

Driving us back to the hotel, Hass, unprovoked, began to speak:

"She left the city, went somewhere in the mountains when it happened. But she said she would come down today to meet you. I don't know what happened. I will keep ringing the number I have."

"Give me the number," Mona said suddenly.

This seemed to fluster Hass. "Well," he said. "I think it's best if I call. She's very frightened. And it's not that simple; every time I have to go through several people to get to her. Like I said, she's very frightened."

He dropped us off and left. As soon as we were in the room, Mona became more agitated.

"None of this makes sense," she said, lighting a cigarette and smacking the lighter onto the glass-topped bedside table. "Who is this woman, anyway? And how did the news-paper get the news before we did?"

I reminded her of what the police inspector had said, that the journalist from *La Tribune* was the first on the scene.

"Yes, but who called him?"

She spent the next few hours telephoning Father's friends. Taleb was not home, but Hydar answered. They spoke for a long time. As soon as she hung up, before I had a chance to ask what he had told her, the telephone rang. It was Taleb. They spoke late into the night. I slept on the sound of her voice telling him what happened, what Hass said, what the police said. And late into the night the tele-phone rang again. It must have been someone else, because she had to repeat the whole story.

× × ×

In the morning she said, "I can't stand this place," and in-sisted we breakfast somewhere else rather than at the hotel. We found a nearby café. And although it was a cold day, she wanted to sit outside.

"This is better," she said when we sat in our coats at a small round table on the edge of the empty pavement. "Everywhere else, I feel people are listening."

Then she stared fixedly at a spot in the distance. She seemed determined. I wondered what Taleb, Hydar and whoever it was who had called in the middle of the night had told her—what they thought happened to Father and what they thought she and I should do.

Very faint in the distance, there was the sound of drums and discordant trumpets. Now the music seemed a street or two away.

"We need someone high up," she said.

Then we saw them: girls and boys dressed in blue uniforms with gold fringes, crashing cymbals, blowing horns that gleamed white in the winter light. Those inside the café came out onto the pavement and stood right behind us. Mona leaned over and shouted in my ear:

"A minister, someone like that."

People looked down from windows here and there, clapping, waving. Each face was smiling. It was not even 9:00 a.m. yet. For some reason the spectacle of a marching band amid these cold gray buildings was disturbing. When I looked at Mona, I found her face covered behind her hands, the fingers pressed tightly together. Was she crying or laughing? The sound was now deafening; it pressed against my chest. Some of the young musicians smiled toward us. The idea of smiling back was impossible. When I turned to Mona again, she was gone. Her bag was not there either. I could not see her anywhere. I faced the band again. The large bass drums were now passing. One of the girls placed a hand on the arm of the boy beside her and let it brush down his sleeve. He smiled without needing to look at her. And gradually the sound diminished. The square blue backs of the last row, crossed with the white belts of the large barrel drums, disappeared round the bending street. The heads in the apartment windows above were no longer there. And the pavement was once again empty. There was still no sign of Mona.

I asked the waiter if he had seen her.

"In the toilet," he said, then, "Don't worry, she'll be back."

I wondered if he was making fun of me.

A few minutes later she was standing beside me, her bag on her shoulder, ready to leave.

× × ×

We returned to the hotel.

"A man came asking for you," the hotel receptionist said when we collected our key. "No, madame, he didn't leave a name. He waited for a few minutes, then left."

I was sure it was Hass, but a little hope lingered. I could not wait for Mona to finish washing her face. I dialed his number.

"Thank God," he said when he heard my voice. "I couldn't find you anywhere. The hotel had no idea where you were; they said you had missed breakfast. I went to the police station; they said you hadn't been there."

"Here's Mona," I told him when I saw her come out of the bathroom. "It's Hass."

She wrapped a hand over the receiver so tightly that the blood left her knuckles.

"Was it him who came earlier?" she whispered.

I nodded.

"Hass, was that you who came to the hotel?" she said without saying hello. "I just felt like a walk. Listen, I have been thinking," she said, facing her lap. "I want to see the journalist. . . . What do you mean, why? Because he was there before anyone else—" she said and stopped as if interrupted.

She looked at me then turned slightly away. I watched her rib cage swell and recede.

"Listen, what are you afraid of? . . . Then call the fucking journalist," she said and hung up, keeping her hand on the receiver.

She collected her sunglasses, address book and cigarettes, throwing them carelessly into her bag.

"Come on," she said. "We're going back to the station."

At the hotel lobby I stopped and ran back to the room. I shoved the plastic bag that contained Father's things into my suitcase, deep beneath the clothes.

Out on the street, walking beside her, I worried about what she would do next. It was an odd feeling: I feared for her but could not say from what.

Inspector Martin Durand did not make us wait. He led us back to the same sparsely furnished room.

"Have you distributed his photograph to the border crossings?" Mona asked.

"We are doing all we can," Martin Durand said.

"Whoever abducted him is trying to take him abroad."

"The border police have been notified."

"Not good enough; you must give them this photograph."

"I know this must be awful for you. I can't imagine. But you must know that we are doing all we can."

I could see that he found Mona's conviction that Father's abductors would want to take him out of Switzerland suspicious.

"There is a good chance," I said, "he was taken by our country. I mean by the people who now run our country."

"Not 'a good chance': hundred percent," Mona snapped.

Martin Durand looked at her, then at me.

CHAPTER 20

Mona ordered sandwiches from room service for lunch. As we ate, she called Monsieur Hass's office at least three times, and every time his polite secretary informed her that he was in a meeting. She asked me to call, to pretend to be someone else. I got the same response. A few minutes later the telephone rang. I answered it.

"May I speak to Madame Mona?" He sounded tired. "I am sorry, I have been busy," he voluntarily explained.

As soon as she took the receiver Mona said, "Where on earth have you been?" Then, before he could have possibly had a chance to explain, she said, "Right, well, listen. Have you contacted the journalist? . . . What do you mean, he's out of town? Isn't he meant to be a local reporter? How convenient: on holiday. And did you get hold of that woman? Or has she bloody disappeared too?"

Barely an hour passed before the receptionist called to say a Monsieur Hass was here. We could not possibly receive him in our tiny room, now smelling of food, so we went down. We found him pacing, his shoes making a high-pitched crack every time they hit the tiles. The three of us sat in the corner of the hotel lounge.

"You and I know he hasn't just run off," Mona said softly.

He looked at me with concern.

"Nuri," Mona said. "Can you please fetch my address book from upstairs?"

When I returned I approached slowly from behind the sofa where they were sitting, catching some of their conversation.

"They have a responsibility to protect him. They can't brush it under the carpet."

"Let me see what I can do," he said.

When they saw me they stood up.

"All right then," she said. "You will call me."

"Yes, as soon as I get hold of my friend."

I followed her to the lift. She stood just inside the sliding doors. When they drew shut she spoke.

"Decent fellow, that man," she said. "He just needs a good kick up the backside."

The doors opened, and she marched through them.

I tried to understand what was going on. I asked whom Hass was going to call.

"Someone he knows at the Federal Department of Home Affairs."

"What's that?"

"Their equivalent of the Home Office."

"What, like the police?"

"Above the police."

She lay down, crossing her hands over her stomach.

"I am going to close my eyes for a few minutes," she said.

I did not know where to go. I thought I could look out of the window, but the view was of the back of the neighboring building.

"The curtains," she suddenly said, her eyes still closed.

I drew them. The room became oddly dark, as if light were an actual solid substance that had poured out of the room. I shut myself into the windowless bathroom but did not turn on the light. I felt my way to the edge of the bathtub. I descended into its dry black shape. I did not cry. I remained there until I heard the telephone ring. I quickly got out.

"Good, you got hold of him," she said, sitting up in bed. "I don't care that it's Christmas. We need to see him. . . . Then why don't I call him?" she said. She stood up. "OK, OK, then you call him now and tell him that if the minister does not see us tomorrow, I will call every paper in Switzerland and tell them that the Swiss government doesn't give a shit about the disappearance of a man who has done nothing but call for the freedom of his people." She listened for a while, then laughed. "Yes, exactly, tell them his wife is crazy. . . . OK, great, I am waiting by the phone," she said and hung up.

For some reason, listening to these words, the easy yet excited voice with which she spoke them, made me feel unsteady. I sat on the floor, my head dangling between my knees.

"What's the matter?" she said.

I shook my head, blinking hard to erase the tiny white blotches.

She lit a cigarette. The smoke quickly filled the room. She yanked the curtains apart but did not open the window.

When the telephone rang again, she let it ring a couple of times before answering it.

"Hi," she said, then, "Good, good. Great, it worked. What time shall we set off? . . . OK, we'll expect you by noon tomorrow. . . . No, he should definitely come. They need to see his son."

She hung up.

"The bastards," she said, underneath her breath.

The light through the window was weak. She began brushing her hair.

"What shall we do for supper?" she said.

× × ×

The following morning Mona and I were back at the station. Inspector Martin Durand would not come out to see us. A woman with a thick neck and eyes so clear that the white in them was as colorless as chalk stood in a uniform behind the counter and told us to come back another time.

"I'm not leaving until he comes out and speaks to me," Mona said.

"Madame, Monsieur Durand is not here."

"We will wait," Mona said and sat down in one of the chairs against the wall.

After ten minutes or so the inspector came out and told her, his face growing red with the words, "Please know we are doing all we can. We will call you, I promise, as soon as we have news." No matter what Mona said after that he would repeat the same words, with less emotion yet more finality, adding, "I am sorry," in the beginning, and sometimes at the end, and other times, oddly, in the middle. Mona by now looked defeated. It was then that I lost my temper.

"Can't you see this is dangerous?" I kept repeating in a voice that caught me off guard.

The inspector stared at me from behind the counter.

Mona took hold of one of my arms and led me out onto the street. The veins in her neck bulged with every breath. I watched her cry. She pressed a pale hand against her forehead. Her eyes peered wildly, and her mouth opened until the hand on her brow came down to cover it. She looked at me furiously, as if I were responsible, as if I were suddenly a stranger to her. But I must have misread all of this, because then she placed a hand on my shoulder and said, "Don't cry, my darling." We began to walk slowly down the street. She held her shoulders tightly together, as if the rest of her body might break loose and collapse to the ground. The dark maroon bag that usually rested against her side was now elbowed back, its soft leather beating against her ribs. Then, without a word or looking to see if I was still there, she turned in to a café. She sat down at a small square table beside a column, leaving her handbag on the table. With a trembling hand she pulled out a cigarette. The waiter came over and stood motionless beside us. Mona did not react. I asked him to bring her a cup of coffee. She lifted her eyes, asking, "What?" then looked at the waiter and said, "Yes, coffee, please." The man turned to me, and I heard myself say, "The same," although I had never had coffee before. A long minute or two passed. Then she remembered something. She searched in her bag, pulled out the address book and took it to the telephone in the corner of the café.

"Who are you going to call?" I asked.

She did not look at me. All I could hear from her conversation was the occasional *s*.

Who was she talking to: Hass, Taleb, Hydar, or some other friend or associate Father had introduced her to? She hung up and returned to the table.

"We must leave. Immediately. Apparently we, too, are in danger. Might be needed to convince him to talk."

Now the fear I had felt standing in front of Béatrice Benameur's building began to make sense. Of course—why would those who stole Father not want the rest of us? Before I could ask who had told her this, she was on her way back to the telephone. She dialed a number, waved to the waiter, asked him a question, then impatiently handed him the receiver.

"Charlie's on his way," she said, taking her seat and lighting another cigarette.

"Who's Charlie?"

"Hass."

She waved to the waiter again. "You gave him the address?"

"Yes, madame."

"Good," she said, handing him some money. "Please bring the change straightaway."

A few minutes later Hass walked into the café.

"We need to get on the first flight out," she told him.

His eyes became alive with a sort of purposeful intelligence. I was sure this was how he looked whenever Father entrusted him with an important task.

Mona stood up, but he waved her down. He ordered a coffee.

"What are you doing?" she asked.

Without saying a word, he went to the telephone.

When he returned he said, "A couple of minutes."

He drank his coffee in silence. Then the telephone in the corner of the café began ringing. The waiter answered it and handed the receiver to Hass.

"My secretary found two seats on a midnight flight. This way we will have time for our appointment."

He drove us to the hotel and waited outside until we packed. Mona asked me to put on a white shirt.

CHAPTER 21

It took one and a half hours to drive to Bern. We were silent most of the way, as if each one of us were trying to settle some overworked valve in our head. When we entered Bern, Hass leaned slightly toward Mona and in a near whisper said, "Like I told you, the minister is busy, but we will meet his aide and my friend who is a member of parliament." Then he added as an afterthought: "It's a spectacular building."

He parked in a side street, and we walked. When the large dark-stone building was in view, he pointed enthusiastically to it and said, "See what I mean?"

We looked up at the arches stacked maybe three or four stories high. Two square towers stood on either side, each with a small red flag on top. It did not seem spectacular at all but silly and overbearing, like a square-jawed bodyguard.

I moved closer to Mona, relieved that she did not respond to his question.

A woman holding a purple spiral-bound notebook with brightly colored stickers on it led us through a long, polished hallway and up a grand staircase that was as wide as a car. Every so often she would look back to make sure we were still behind her. Eventually the wood-paneled corridors turned white, fluorescent lights replaced the chandeliers. We arrived at a room that looked like a classroom. It even had a blackboard on one wall. The three of us sat on one side of the long white table that stood in the middle. In the center of the table there was a jug full of water but with only two empty glasses beside it. I was thirsty but did not pour myself a glass. After a few minutes the same woman with the childish notebook walked in, followed by a man dressed in a dark-blue suit and bright red tie. He greeted Hass warmly while the woman watched and smiled.

"We were at university together," Hass explained.

"I am very sorry to hear what happened," he told Mona.

He shook my hand but without looking in my eyes.

He and the woman sat opposite us, with an empty chair between them.

"The minister's aide is on her way," the man said.

"Very kind of you to see us at such short notice," Mona said.

"We want to do everything we can," he said.

Then a tall woman walked in, shook the hand of each one of us and quickly took her seat in the middle. She looked at the woman beside her, who opened her notebook and held her pen at the top of an empty page.

"The minister apologizes. He wanted to see you personally as soon as he heard. But, as you might appreciate, he is very busy."

"Of course," Mona said softly, which surprised me.

"We have read the police report and the statement you gave to Monsieur Durand, so I won't trouble you with repeating the story, but, like you, we are very concerned indeed."

She had slim, elongated features. I was somehow sure she had her father's face. Her arms were nearly as white as the table and completely hairless. The color altered a little at the hands: there was a hint of green to the heels of her palms, the knuckles were pink, but the fingertips were unhappily red, as if she spent a great deal of time washing dishes.

"My husband is a regular visitor to your country," Mona said. "If something has happened to him it will be a scandal."

None of the faces opposite reacted to this.

"You are meant to protect your visitors."

"Like I said, we are very concerned," the minister's aide repeated. "The border police, as well as the intelligence services, have been notified."

The water jug had tiny silver balls of air clinging to its sides. I wondered how long it had been standing there: how many days or weeks or even months.

"Would you like some water?" the woman taking notes said.

"Yes, sorry, I should have asked earlier," the man said and stood up.

He did not have a belt on, and, although his fly was done up, he had missed the last short distance to the button. The zipper there widened like the open mouth of a small fish. He poured the water quickly, straightening the jug just before the water reached the rim. He placed one glass in front of Mona and the other in front of me. I had intended to drink mine in one go but could not take more than a sip.

"What I feel we must prepare for," the minister's aide said as she looked at her colleagues, "is the possibility that he was driven to one of the neighboring countries. France or Italy for example. It's not unusual for our immigration officials not to check papers of those leaving the country."

Mona made a strange sound, like a short wheeze. Everyone else must have noticed, but no one said anything.

"Is that what you think happened to my father?" I asked.

"No, we are just saying that it's a possibility," the man said.

I looked at Mona but she did not react.

"This is the fourth day," she finally said.

And no one else spoke after that. Not until the woman with the notebook, who had filled a few pages by now, said, "So, to recap: we will make sure that all border-crossing stations are aware of this and will notify the authorities of the neighboring countries also."

× × ×

At the airport Hass did something unexpected. After kissing Mona on both cheeks, he hugged me. The edges of his eyelids, where a woman would wear her kohl, were as red as a fresh wound.

"Don't worry," he told her. "I will follow up with the police."

When we were a few paces away, he shouted after us.

"Call if you need anything, anything at all."

We got on an indirect flight home. We had a few hours in Athens. We tried to sleep on the airport benches. I watched her cheek pressed against her wrist. She seemed as foreign to me then as the figures that passed us in the airport lounge.

CHAPTER 22

We landed in Cairo in the early morning. The damp tarmac shone under the streetlights. The air was heavy with the human smell of the old and overpopulated city. I had never felt so deeply disoriented. Mother came into my thoughts. My need for her was sudden, bottomless and unendurable.

In the apartment, before we slept, Mona opened a can of tuna and heated a couple of loaves of frozen bread, nearly burning them. We ate in silence. I was not occupied by the obvious question of what happened to Father but by the physical need to be beside him.

In the morning, as soon as Naima arrived, she asked, "Where is the pasha?"

"Working," Mona told her.

"Is he all right? Because, yesterday alone, Ustaz Nuri's aunts, Madam Souad and Madam Salwa, called at least ten times. They said they'd heard bad news but wouldn't say what."

Later that day I heard Naima open the door and let someone in. I rushed to see who it was and found Taleb standing in the hall.

Mona pulled him into the sitting room.

"The regime—" he said, then stopped. When he resumed, he spoke his words quickly and in a near whisper, as if he could not wait to get to the other side. "The regime has issued a statement saying they have him, that he has, of his own volition, returned to the capital. But they didn't show him. They could be bluffing. It's possible."

As he delivered these words, Taleb leaned toward Mona. When she neither spoke nor lifted her eyes from her hands, he looked at me and said, "I came as soon as I heard."

× × ×

For the rest of the day and whenever I was alone, Naima would follow me, asking, "What happened? Where is the pasha? I know something is wrong."

In the end I told her. Panic and fear were in her eyes, but her voice remained reasonable and steady.

"Look, your father often did this. His work demands it. It has happened before."

"Really?"

"Yes, many times. He would vanish for days, and your mother, God have mercy on her, would become sick with worry, but before long he was at the door as if nothing had happened."

She tried to smile. She held me and I let her.

"You should call your aunts," she said suddenly.

She fetched a number written in her own large hand.

Aunt Salwa said I should come immediately to live with them, then she began to cry. Aunt Souad took the receiver.

"Nuri, habibi, listen very carefully," she said. "Ask your stepmother to put you on the first plane home, here where you belong. Don't be frightened; no one will touch you; they are only interested in your father. This is your country."

"But I have school," I said.

"Give me your stepmother," she said.

I sat beside Mona.

"I understand your concern," Mona said, then waited patiently. "Yes, I understand." My heart began to beat wildly. "Listen—" she said and was interrupted. I watched her cheeks turn red. "Auntie, please, you are being unreasonable. . . . No, you listen to me. I know I am only twenty-eight, but I am capable of looking after Nuri. Disrupting his education now would be hugely irresponsible. Thank you very much," she said and hung up, her breath swelling the square sail of skin at the base of her neck. The telephone rang again. "Don't answer it," she told Naima.

I followed her to where Taleb was sitting at the dining table.

"What's the matter?" he asked.

"Nothing," she said and sat down.

I placed my hand over hers, hoping she would hold it tightly.

× × ×

When it came time to sleep, and regardless of how much I insisted, Taleb would not take my bed. Mona stood by, saying nothing; so did Naima, which was when I understood that because Father was not home, it would have been improper for Taleb, being a single man, to sleep in the room next to Mona's bedroom. Naima spread a sheet on the couch in the living room and brought him a blanket. He lay in his clothes. I sat on the floor beside him. I told him what Naima had told me, that this had happened before. He placed a hand on my head but did not say anything.

"Uncle Taleb, when do you think Baba will return?"

"I don't know."

"Do you think it will take a long time?"

"I don't know."

I began to cry.

"Your father is brave," he said.

I could not understand what that had to do with anything.

"You have to be just as brave."

He took hold of my hand as if we were about to cross a main road.

"I was with him in the hospital when you were born. I had never seen a bigger smile. He took me by the shoulders, nearly crushed my bones. And every test you passed, every new sport you started, he mentioned it in his letters."

This surprised me. I had always had the persistent feeling that I was a disappointment.

"There was nothing you could do wrong. When you got accepted at that famous English boarding school, he called me. He was so proud."

I wiped away the tears. My eyelids were heavy. A while later I felt his hand on my shoulder.

"Go to bed."

After brushing my teeth I came back to ask, "Do you have to leave tomorrow?"

"Yes. But if you ever need me, I will fly back." When I did not move, he said, "Here," and handed me a piece of paper on which he had written, carefully and meticulously, his full name, telephone number and address.

CHAPTER 23

The following night, long after Taleb had left for the airport and Naima had left on her long commute home, I heard a clank in Father's study. It sounded like a nut cracking. I found Mona ransacking the drawers, wild with impatience. I went after her, ordered the papers and pushed shut a couple of drawers, then stopped. I watched her body bend and twist beneath the nightdress. I sat in Father's padded desk chair. It was too big for me. The backrest that reached his shoulders was taller than my head. My eyes fell on the raincoat hanging behind the door, the fabric sculpting the ghostly shape of Father's shoulders. I left the room. I paced up and down the corridor and when she eventually came out of the study I stared at her, and she said, with a voice as hard as a stick, "No, you won't. You can't blame me for this."

x x x

Hass called daily, trying to reassure us that he was still following up with the Swiss authorities.

"I was in Bern again yesterday," he would sometimes say before asking to speak to Mona.

I would sit beside her. She let me listen in on those calls, happy sometimes even to lean slightly toward me. Other times she would press the receiver tightly against her ear and point to the packet of cigarettes that was not entirely out of her reach, asking me to fetch it.

The minister's aide had refused to give the journalist from *La Tribune de Genève* an interview. "They said better results could be achieved by not generating too much publicity," Hass told Mona. "Clearly wary of getting involved in any kind of international trouble," he had said.

He was also still trying to trace Béatrice Benameur. There was no answer when he called at her flat or rang the number he had for her.

"It's obvious," Mona told him. "She was part of the kidnapping."

Hass did not respond.

x x x

Often before falling asleep I would lie in the black room and fantasize about how one day I would find Béatrice Benameur and take my revenge. I still remember the sound of my heart keeping me awake.

The telephone continued to ring incessantly. Then after a few days it grew quiet. Relatives and neighbors who might have filled the chairs in the hall if Father had died were silent in the face of his disappearance. Even my aunts and Taleb stopped calling so much. A great emptiness began to fill the place of my father. It became unbearable to hear his name. It must have been the same for Mona, for she, too, hardly mentioned him now. At times it was almost possible to imagine that he had never existed. Yet every morning, the moment I opened my eyes, I believed he was there, that I would find him sitting at the dining table, holding a cup of coffee in the air as he looked down at the folded newspaper on his lap.

× × ×

As if expecting his vanishing at any moment, Father had drafted a will with the meticulousness of a heart surgeon. Neither Mona nor I had known of its existence. We found it when we managed to open the safe in the corner of the study.

I had secretly hoped to find a note explaining everything: his disappearance, instructions on where to find him, instructions on how to live. I had even allowed myself to hope to read, finally, an explanation for Mother's sudden passing. Instead, we found his will sealed in an envelope, the insignia of a floating olive tree, its roots dangling in midair, embossed on the top center. After Father could no longer return home he had commissioned this design and had had it stamped on his stationery.

The will, effective in the event of "death or disappearance," left Mona three hundred thousand pounds sterling, "to be discharged in ten equal installments of thirty thousand paid annually." The rest was to go to "my only son, Nuri el-Alfi."

Why did he add "my only son"? I wondered. Did he think anyone would suggest otherwise?

Monsieur Charlie Hass, who held the original copy of the will, was to "fully administer the inheritance" until I reached eighteen, and then "administrate it partially" until I was twenty-four, when I would become "in complete charge of my inheritance." Between the ages of eighteen and twenty-four, in order to qualify for my allowance, I had to be engaged in studies leading to a PhD, "in any subject except business or political science, because both politics and business benefit from an indirect education." I remembered how Father used to say "a man must not take up employment until he has completed his education." He could not understand why some well-to-do families encouraged their sons to work summers. "How is a young man to know himself if he is required to plunge into the first job offered him? Humility is not earned through humiliation." And so I could not secure any form of employment, "voluntary or otherwise," until twenty-four, when I could do whatever I pleased, according to my father.

× × ×

I hid the police plastic bag that contained Father's last things in my wardrobe. I dreaded Mona asking me about it.

I could not imagine ever parting with it. I did not dare unseal the bag again but spent hours with the newspaper article, rereading it, studying every part of the photograph, not only the features of Béatrice Benameur but everything else contained in the frame. I discovered things I had not noticed before. Then I saw something that had me reeling for days afterward. It looked like a corner of a baby's crib. I showed it to Naima.

"But that is a chair, Ustaz Nuri," she said, continuing to peer into the picture.

By the evening I had convinced myself she was right. It was only a shawl resting on a ladder-back chair.

× × ×

There is a moment in the Cairo day when the sun seems to hover motionless. In the days that followed, I would sit beside Mona at the dining table, watching the fading light bounce off the Nile and paint her neck fiery red. Suddenly her beauty would look sorrowful: a fruit bruising in front of my eyes. The sun would roll off the horizon and leave the river mute and gray. It was difficult then to imagine the light ever returning. A smog-stained cloud would enter the sky. Naima would creep up from behind and switch on the lamps. Only then could you feel the pain and longing ease and it was possible then to play a game of cards.

Cards became our nightly ritual. And I let her win most times. She was terrible at chess and backgammon, but in poker she could hold her own. Sometimes, when she was really restless, I would beat her, and she would turn wonderfully competitive and ask Naima, who hated to touch the bottle, to bring over the brandy.

"I mustn't let this boy get the better of me."

Which made Naima blush and say, "May God preserve the goodwill, madam."

One such evening, after Naima had washed the dinner plates, placed the bottle with a hand gloved in a kitchen rag on the table and left on her long journey home, I let Mona win several games in a row and watched her sink a quarter of the brandy. She turned up an English song and began to dance around the room. Then she said, "You like to watch me, don't you?" She came close and into my eyes whispered, "You are a strange boy. If I let you, you would spend a lifetime watching me."

I must have turned red, because she laughed; she laughed and I did not know where to look.

She went to her room. I expected not to see her until morning, but then she called me. She had changed into one of the short cotton dresses she slept in. She looked like a girl dressed in an adult's T-shirt.

"Put on your pajamas and come tell me a story," she said.

I made something up, a story about my father. And although I felt guilty doing it, I excluded any mention of the woman Mona had never met, her rival, my mother. At one point in my story, which was about a walk Father and I had never taken around the oasis at Fayoum, eating grapes, she closed her eyes and smiled.

"The sun was shining, but not harshly," I told her.

She nodded.

With every breath her nipples pressed against the thin cotton. Her smiling lips glistened under the brush of the bedside lamp. I had no doubt. My heart thundered as if it were a thing trapped. But my courage went only as far as running my fingers along my own lips. Just then she opened her eyes and they fell heavily on my mouth. Unlike mine, her body did not seem to lag behind her thoughts. She rose and kissed me on the lips. Had the brandy put her in a dream state? Were the lips she kissed my father's? I never knew that horror and delight could be so sweet and potent. She reached behind her and turned off the light. I felt her arms pulling me to her chest, then the hot breath of her sigh burn my forehead. For a moment I changed my mind. There was no fire, and the house was not full of smoke, but I wanted to push her away and run to the window and let the air wash my lungs. But I remained slack and willing in her arms until the moment passed and sleep overtook me.

The next time I surfaced I found that the night had wrapped us even tighter, coiled her bare thigh round my waist and pushed mine up between her legs. Like branches of a tree, each limb had found its natural way. And although the shame was powerful, it remained distant. I moved against her and she moved with me. It must have been a cloudy night because the yellow city lights reflected off the sky and entered the room. I saw her eyes blink in the weak sepia.

CHAPTER 24

The sun did return. A stab of light was piercing through
the window. Countless tiny fragments floated in its path.
Every day it comes, this sun, newborn and fierce. I thanked
God for the morning. I lay unmoving, tempering my breath,
until Naima rang the doorbell. Mona sat up on the side of
the bed, pulled a hand through her hair, then turned around
and looked at me. She went to open the door.

Naima served breakfast then disappeared to tidy the bed-
rooms. There was only one bed to make. I wondered, if confronted, how we would explain that. She returned to the
dining room and glanced at Mona.

I felt guilty the whole day. I became short with Mona.
And she in turn became motherly, sitting on the edge of my
bed, asking if I should not be reading a book. Then her eyes
fell on my fingers.

"Your nails are too long. Here," she said and ran to fetch the nail clipper.

That night I lay in my bed praying death would take me. In the middle of the night I was walking the apartment, wading through that peculiar stillness in which everything seemed possible: Mother's voice, Father's steps. I decided that by morning I would suggest to Mona that we close the apartment and move to London or Geneva or Alexandria or even Nordland—anywhere but here.

I went to her and found her spread on her back, taking long, deep breaths. I had the thought of strangling her. But then I wanted to kiss her, kiss her so hard as to suck the breath out of her. I lay beside her, but she went on sleeping. I pulled the covers over us. I crawled between her legs and there made myself as small as possible. I was on my side, my head near her groin and my knees in my chest. She hummed but did not stir. Now I could smell her. And the smell surprised me: moist and round, like your palms after a long hot day's cycling. Then she was awake. It was a cloudless night, but still I could just about make out her face looking down at me, helpless in the dark.

× × ×

Over breakfast the following morning I could not stop myself from watching her. She did her best to avoid my gaze, pulling tighter the wings of her dressing gown. There was nothing mysterious now about those breasts. Her nipples were like wilted grapes.

This time Naima was not only throwing glances but also setting the plates down noisily.

"What's the matter with you?"

"This is wrong, Ustaz Nuri." Then to Mona, "Wrong!"

Mona flinched.

I had never heard Naima shout before. She ran off to the kitchen crying. I heard her say, "It's my fault. Forgive me, Kamal Pasha."

"What's the matter with her?" I asked, and shouted, "Naima."

"Listen," Mona said quietly.

"Naima, I am calling you."

"You have to respect my wishes, Ustaz," Naima said softly, as if I were there beside her in the kitchen. The belated insertion of Ustaz in the end brought on an aggressive melancholy that tied my tongue and made me want to rush to her, kiss her hands, beg forgiveness.

"Listen," Mona repeated.

I could not stop the tears.

"I am sorry, Nuri, truly sorry. It has barely been a month and look how badly I am coping. I will be better, I promise. I have decided to move back to England, to be near you."

Naima saw I was crying. She stood by the kitchen counter watching me.

Mona took a deep breath and seemed older all of a sudden.

"I will move to London. You will visit me there."

"But you said you loved the English countryside."

Her eyes blinked slowly like gates closing. Then, looking toward Naima, and in her broken Arabic, she said, "This time I will not fail."

"I can help you. I can move to a school in London. I hate Daleswick."

She shook her head again, tried to smile.

× × ×

After breakfast I listened to her showering. At one point she hummed a tune, then stopped. I wondered whether she had bent to scrub her shins or had suddenly thought, Be quiet, silly woman; this is no time for singing.

I returned to the dining table, pretending I had not left my seat. She emerged dressed and perfumed, the apartment keys jingling off the medallion in her hand. She went into the kitchen and without a word hugged Naima and kissed her on both cheeks. Naima instinctively bowed and kissed Mona's hand.

"Do we need anything from the shops? I will be back soon," she said and walked out.

After a few seconds I rushed to the door and caught her stepping into the lift.

"Where are you going?"

She held a hand out and the sliding doors shuddered back. "To the doctor," she whispered.

"Why?"

"It's nothing, darling. Just a bad headache."

I went to Father's study and felt a panic at sitting in his chair. The room looked undisturbed. Naima—or, who knows, perhaps even Mona—must have come in and closed all the drawers and placed every object where it belonged. Father had left a book on the desk, with a page folded a quarter of the way in. I could pick up where he left off, I thought.

× × ×

On the morning of my departure, Naima scrubbed the fridge door, although it looked perfectly clean. She did not respond when I said good morning, and whenever I came close her body hardened. Mona seemed impatient with Naima's behavior. She kept saying, "You will see him soon," which even Naima knew was a lie.

"Perhaps we should say goodbye here," Mona said.

I stood beside my suitcase. Abdu, in his modest and quiet manner, crept soundlessly from behind and removed the luggage.

"No, that is not a good idea," Mona then said, more to herself.

Naima stood still, her soapy hands clasped together. Her figure looked as stiff and precarious as a reed in water. I wandered over to her. She hugged me. There was nothing more convincing than Naima's embrace.

Mona and I sat in the back of the car. She looked out of

the window, and I pretended to do the same. Abdu was also silent. He pulled the seat belt across his chest and looked at me in the rearview mirror. Although I could not see his entire face I knew he was trying to smile. Just then we heard Naima's breathless plea.

"Wait."

She got in the front passenger seat, and the usual argument ensued. But this time Naima did not resist for long. She did what she was told and fastened the seat belt. Every so often she would turn, take my hand and kiss it three or four times.

In the departure lounge the sheets of marble and glass amplified every sound.

"Call as soon as you arrive," Mona said.

"What will happen to Naima?" I asked in English.

"Her salary will continue until we see what happens. And the same with Abdu."

And when she spotted a tear filling my eye, she said, "It's better this way. I will come see you as soon as I settle in London, if not before."

And even though I recognized tenderness in her manner, I wondered if this was not punishment for what had taken place the night before.

She and I embraced. She let go before I did, then awkwardly tried to hug me again.

"OK, young man," Abdu said, and we shook hands.

Naima hugged me too tightly. She held my face in her hands. They were unusually cold.

"Promise you will never forget me."

She rubbed her wrists, brought a hand to her neck and left it there. She turned to Abdu, looking at him as if hoping for rescue.

Waiting in line, I could feel their gaze on my back, the weight of it. I spotted a man closed in behind glass partitioning, sitting at an empty desk and looking out of the window. Behind him and farther away from the window, a woman sat on a chair against the wall. She, too, was looking out of the window. The light paled their faces. There was a tender quality to their stillness. Then she moved, took out two sandwiches and handed him one. She might have been his wife or perhaps his sister visiting during the lunch hour. The world had to be sliced into hours to fill; otherwise you could go mad with loneliness.

I turned around and saw that they were gone. Lines stretched in all directions. I smelled my father: his musky, warm skin. I looked about and, even though he was not there, the smell persisted.

CHAPTER 25

It was late January, winter just as dominant as it was when I left for Switzerland. I had been gone only six weeks, but it felt like an entire lifetime had passed. At Heathrow I had to force myself down to the Underground station. My heart was as tight as a knot. And when I boarded the train at St. Pancras and the door was shut, the racing pulse returned. I could not look anyone in the eye. My fingers were ice cold, the color beneath the nails white. I watched the fast-skipping fields. When the cab pulled up the long gravel path to my boardinghouse I saw that, despite everything, nothing at Daleswick had changed.

I was late by two weeks and felt overwhelmed by the amount of work I had to catch up on. Mr. Galebraith had telephoned Cairo after the first day of absence. Mona told him that I was ill. "Terrible flu," I heard her say.

"So is it true or were you just skiving off?" Alexei asked.

"Actually," I said, feeling my heart rise, "I wasn't ill. Don't tell anyone, but it was my father." When he did not immediately respond I added, "But he's fine now."

× × ×

Two months later Mona called to say she was in London.

"Where are you staying?"

"With a friend until I find a place."

I wondered if, late into the night, she had confided in this nameless friend what had taken place between her and her stepson in Cairo.

"Who is your friend?"

"Someone I know from university."

What she said next seemed a deliberate attempt to change the subject.

"I miss you. Are you well? How's school?"

"What did you do with Naima?"

"I had to let her go."

"And her salary?"

"I tried, but she refused. Tearful and proud. A good soul. In the end I gave the money to Abdu, who is much more pragmatic, of course. He will give it to her when she is less emotional."

"How much?"

"The equivalent of three months."

When I did not say anything she said, "We'll talk when I see you."

× × ×

A couple of days later, while I was eating lunch, Mr. Watson, the maths teacher, zigzagged all the way to the opposite end of the dining hall, where I happened to be sitting that day, and bent close to my ear, causing everyone at the long table to look up.

"You have a guest waiting in the headmaster's office." A quick, sympathetic grin passed across his face.

Although I knew who the guest must be, I could not resist the possibility that I might find standing in the headmaster's office not Mona but my father, altered, perhaps thinner, less certain, older and, although it was a perfectly sunny day, wrapped in the same raincoat that was hanging behind the door of his study. The desire to cling to this hope, coupled with the possibility of finding a changed man, did not speed my progress; I walked slowly, my hand tracing the wood-paneled walls.

The headmaster's door was open. I could see him sitting behind his desk, his figure darkened by the large windows on either side, facing someone out of view. When I came close I saw that opposite the desk, a couple of meters away, far enough that anything spoken was in danger of being overheard, sat Mona. The sunlight that poured in through one of the windows landed on the carpeted floor just short of her chair, but somehow the edges of her hair were burnished by it. The headmaster's head moved. Mona turned. She smiled. Now I could see Mr. Galebraith, leaning on a bookcase in the corner. His tie was loose around the fastened collar. He seemed worried.

"Come in," the headmaster said.

I did and when I was a step or two away from Mona I heard Mr. Galebraith close the door behind me.

I did not want to embrace Mona in front of the two men. I extended my hand and she kissed each one of my cheeks. I detected a new perfume.

The quality of the atmosphere somehow confirmed that she had told them something, but what precisely I was not sure. Did she tell them the truth, that my father and legal guardian had been kidnapped by his political adversaries from the bed of a Swiss woman neither of us knew? Or did she make something up, something simple and tidy for the Englishmen? Did she, for example, tell them that he had fallen critically ill, descended into a coma, that the doctors were pessimistic? Or did she say he had died? Had he died? Had she heard something? The continued silence and the way that they were all looking at me seemed to confirm that the three of them knew something I did not.

Mr. Galebraith was suddenly facing me. He could not have been more than an arm's length away. His eyes softened. The transformation was as subtle as it was mysterious.

"So sorry, old chap," he said.

He had never called me that before.

"Your stepmother has just told us," the headmaster said. "I must say, although you ought to have informed us earlier,

I do admire your discretion. And, in light of it, we have all agreed that, besides Mr. Galebraith and me, no one else needs to know. We are determined to guard your studies and your place among your peers. Education must continue even in the darkest of times."

He got up and, like Mr. Galebraith had done, came and stood in front of me.

"Not a million years ago, fine men like you attended this school while the nation went to war."

He let his hand rest for the briefest of intervals on my shoulder.

"We are hopeful, of course. But in the meantime Mrs. el-Alfi will act as your legal guardian."

CHAPTER 26

Soon after my father disappeared Monsieur Charlie Hass began a regular correspondence with me that was formal and disciplined, sticking to the business that bound us: my inheritance. But in one letter, about a year after my father disappeared, he veered off the usual business line and expressed a perplexingly raw feeling. The letter arrived not with the quarterly bank statement and bill of his charges but on its own, written in a hurried, almost exasperated hand that covered both sides of an A5 notepad piece of paper with a torn, perforated edge. It started: "I have been thinking of you and of how you must be feeling. It's terrible, just terrible. Your father was an excellent man."

I felt a jealous anger at his referring to my father in the past tense, as if he knew more than I did, not only about Father but also about what might have befallen him.

"And how can anyone expect you to know all that he was and all that he did, the people he knew, the people who loved him? But know this: he loved you very much. If you need proof, look at how thoughtfully he arranged your affairs."

He ended it with: "I am sorry to be writing you like this, but I felt compelled." Then he signed his name.

It was well past midnight when, a few weeks after I received the letter, Mr. Galebraith came to wake me.

"El-Alfi," he whispered, his figure black against the light of the corridor. "Phone call. From Geneva. Mr. Hass. Says he is the family lawyer. Says it's important."

Father has been found, I thought. Why else would a Swiss lawyer call at this hour? I did not run but only just managed to walk beside Mr. Galebraith. The telephone was all the way on the ground floor of the old mansion, in a musty corridor tiled in York stone worn to a shine and bulging out of the ground. I held the cold receiver to my ear and waited until Mr. Galebraith reached the end of the corridor.

"Hello?"

"Is this Monsieur Nuri?"

"Yes."

"Oh, I am sorry, did I wake you? I just wanted to make sure that you are all right. You didn't respond to my letter."

I said nothing.

"Did anyone come to see you, asking questions, hassling you?"

"No. Anyone like who?"

"Are you sure? You know you can tell me if they did."

"Mr. Hass, I don't know what you are talking about."

"In that case, very good. If anything like that happens, call me immediately."

×　×　×

Neither Mr. Galebraith nor the headmaster brought up the subject. And I mentioned Father's disappearance to no one. It became my secret.

Some nights, lying in the dark after lights-out, I came close to telling Alexei, but I did not know what words to use. I did not know how to name what had taken place: kidnap, abduction, theft? None of them seemed right. And how was I to answer the questions that would surely follow, about why and who and how and wasn't there anything I could do.

In March, three months after it happened, I had taken a long walk through the hills. Buds wrapped in their velvet caskets clung to the tips of branches. Everything was on the brink of change. For the first time since I had arrived at Daleswick, the English sun warmed my skin. I had been wrong, I thought; I ought to have told Alexei. I pictured us walking through the grove and up the steep hill. We would sit on the craggy boulder there and look out onto the hills rolling and fading into the distance. We would spot our boardinghouse, small enough to hide behind a thumb. And this time we would climb here not for cigarettes and vodka, and not so that he could tell me about his life back in Germany, but to discuss a matter of the utmost importance. I could no longer wait. How ridiculous that I had left it this long, I told myself. The shock and anguish inflicted by the sudden and yet ambiguous loss of my father felt like a weight on my chest. It had never felt heavier. I wanted to roll it off onto the lap of a trusted friend who might help me make sense of it. I walked briskly back.

I could not find him anywhere. Then, just when I began to wonder if this was not a sign, I found him in the common room watching the news. I sat on the far side, tempering my breath. Besides the library, this was the only room where talking was not encouraged. I waited for him to look my way so that I could gesture to him to follow me. I began to take notice of the news item that was holding his attention. A mother had lost a child. He had been playing in the garden. When she looked up from the kitchen sink he was gone. The cameraman zoomed onto her face as she tried to answer the reporter's questions. It was upsetting to witness such intrusion into another's grief. It was as if the camera took delight in the woman's shame. I wondered what Alexei made of it.

"How could you lose your son?" one boy called out and he was shushed down.

Alexei continued to face the screen.

"Stupid," he said softly.

I was not sure if he meant the woman on the TV or the boy who had just spoken. And because no one turned to him or told him to be quiet, I convinced myself that he meant the boy. But then Alexei jutted his chin out toward the television and got up and left the room. I watched the leather seat of his armchair fill with air.

Nothing would be lost, I reasoned, by holding off for a few days.

I remained agitated, uncertain whether to tell him or not, and at the height of my despair I would feel the sweat pool on my chest. One night a storm took hold of the trees outside our dormitory window. I watched them through the glass. The helpless things swung from side to side in the electric light. The mice in the attic above scurried back and forth. The wind moaned and whistled through the window. The rain, which came and went in sheets, was like a thousand fingernails tapping the glass.

"It's nothing, go to sleep," Alexei said when he heard the floorboards squeak.

The next time I woke up the world was a calm place. The leaves had hardly a breeze to contend with. In their stillness they looked exhausted. The trees on the outer perimeter of the grove had either collapsed or split into two. Alexei was fast asleep. He had slept through the rest of the storm. Something about that astonished me. What comfort allows such trust in the world?

The stillness of that morning seemed to confirm my old instinct not to tell Alexei about my father. I made up my mind: I must keep this private. I could not bear the disquiet of another or worse, far worse, to see him fascinated, entertained by the oddity of what had happened. What is a happy German boy with happy parents to know about this?

CHAPTER 27

A couple of months later Alexei ran into the room we shared at Daleswick with a white piece of paper quivering in his hand. I took the letter, but it was in German.

"My father has been offered a job in Düsseldorf. He accepted it. Annalisa can't believe her luck. She will become a day pupil and I will do my final year there. We will all be together again."

He flung his arms around me. I tried to reciprocate the hug.

"Don't you worry, we'll spend summers together."

Soon it was his last day at school. Before he had even gone to sleep he had packed his clothes, books, and records. He was leaving me Rachmaninoff's Sonata for Cello in G Minor because it was then the most beautiful thing I had heard. We vowed to stay in touch.

His parents and Annalisa were coming to collect him. He seemed nervous. Then I heard he was looking for me. He took me to one side.

"Please don't say anything if you notice something unusual about my mother."

I went to the window when I heard a car come up the gravel path. Alexei ran into his father's arms. Annalisa held her hands, waiting patiently to one side, before she, too, embraced him. She did not let go even after he had dropped his arms down. He laughed and held her again. Then his mother came, balancing on a cane. He was careful with her, hugged her softly and let his ear rest lightly on her shoulder. For a few seconds no one moved. When he let go, she leaned the stick against her hip and gestured fast with her hands. He nodded and said something in German, loudly, as if he were addressing someone hiding in the trees beyond. He looked back, and I thought it was time for me to appear. I was overtly conscious of the loud crunching noise my feet were making on the gravel. His mother was the only one who did not speak when I came to shake her hand. I understood then what Alexei had been anxious about and why that one time when he mentioned how much he missed his mother's singing his eyes had welled. His mother, the singer, had completely lost her voice.

× × ×

During my last days in Cairo, before I had returned to school, Taleb had telephoned nearly every day. He would exchange a few words with Naima first, then ask to speak to me.

"How is our young pasha?" he would say.

He usually sounded cheerful. He would speak about the weather or some film he had seen the evening before. He was a great one for exaggerating: something was either fantastic or truly awful. I now wonder whether his tendency to exaggerate was not a screen behind which he hid his anxieties, for even then I sensed that Taleb not only worried about me but felt somehow responsible for what had happened to my father. I understood this, because I, too, felt responsible.

In late January, when I had returned to Daleswick nearly a fortnight after classes started, he began to telephone every Sunday. He visited me several times too. These visits meant a great deal to me because Taleb did not speak English and seemed for all intents and purposes to dislike England.

I told him about Hass's call. He listened and then asked if anyone had approached me about anything.

"Anyone like who?"

"Anyone like anyone," he said. When I did not speak he added, "If anyone does you call me, understand?"

"OK," I said, even though I had no idea what he meant.

He would often ask when I had last seen Mona.

"Recently," I would tell him. "Last week," I would say if he pressed me for a precise time, even though the truth was

I only saw her every four or five weeks when she would come up for just the afternoon.

"Good, good," he would say. "She is a good woman. And Naima, have you called her?"

"No, why?"

"You should call her from time to time."

"Why?"

"It's your duty."

A couple of weeks later he called again.

"Did you call Naima?"

"No."

"Didn't I tell you to call her? You must call her. You can't lose touch with her. She's too important."

"But I don't have her number."

"What do you mean, you don't have her number?"

"I have to go."

"Wait. I will call you back with her number. Don't move. Five minutes."

I waited by the telephone for fifteen minutes then left. The following day Mr. Galebraith came to say I had a call.

"Naima doesn't have a phone, but this is the number of the nearby mechanic. He will fetch her. Give him time. Be patient."

He read me the number then asked me to read it back to him.

"Call now. And listen, from now on call her every week."

"Every week?"

"Well, once a month at least."

I called the mechanic, but after waiting for more than three minutes I hung up.

A week later I called again:

"Don't make me bring her here again for nothing," the mechanic said.

"But I am calling from England; it's expensive."

"Then hang up and call again in fifteen minutes."

After ten minutes I dialed the number.

"He's eager," I heard him tell her.

"But is that him?" Naima asked.

As soon as she heard my voice she went quiet. Only when she spoke again did I realize she was crying. She begged me to call again, to call often.

"What's today?" she asked, then repeated the same question to the mechanic.

"Sunday," I heard him say.

"Sunday?" she said, then to me: "I will be here, beside the telephone, every Sunday, around this time, just in case you feel like calling." When I did not say anything, she added, "I promise the next time I won't cry."

I did not call after that.

CHAPTER 28

I was seventeen by this time and had perfected the art of squeezing some sort of activity into every gap in the school-year calendar. I was fortunate that Daleswick was known for these trips and that, although it was unusual for any one pupil to do this all year round, it was not entirely uncommon for students there to sometimes choose to go traveling together over Easter, Christmas or summer break instead of going home. We went hiking and sailing; we attended music and theater festivals; we worked for charities and took trips for the sole purpose of seeing a significant building or museum and sometimes just one painting or piece of sculpture. My time had suddenly become precious. I remember afternoons when I would run to my room to fit in half an hour of reading before supper. I felt grateful to my good father for having chosen Daleswick and funding what I knew to be a lavish education and, ultimately, a distraction.

All this meant that I rarely needed to visit Mona. She, on the other hand, would occasionally take the train up on Saturdays and get a room in the bed-and-breakfast in the village. She would collect me in a taxi and take me out for lunch. I lost the old thrill. A gate had shut. And she sensed it, because she leaned forward more than she used to and talked more than ever before.

A waitress once asked if we were mother and son. I let her answer.

"Yes," she said, but as soon as she did her cheeks pinked.

One time she telephoned insisting that I come spend the weekend with her. I boarded the train on Friday afternoon and arrived in London when it was dark. The somber country had given way to a triumphant city. A steady rain fell and glowed silver beneath the streetlamps. I would stop and take shelter inside shop fronts, a practice I had up to then regarded as an eccentricity of the British. But there I was, huddled with them: coated figures under a semi-effective canopy, looking out. Every so often a wind would slant the lines of rain. None of us said a word. We made sure our eyes did not meet. If they did we would quickly turn away without a smile or a nod. Looking at us, you might have thought we were avoiding the lives that awaited us at home. Then, without explanation, certainly without the rain stopping, one of us would pull up his or her lapels and continue bravely down the pavement.

I finally located the address in Little Venice. I stood on the opposite side of the canal, looking at the lit windows. Only when I pressed the bell downstairs did I notice how wet I was.

"Come in," I heard her voice say, and then the buzzer went.

She kissed my cheeks, smiled. But there was something wrong. She was in a hurry, uneasy. An old jazz record played a little too loudly. I had never known her to like that kind of music. Then I spotted a man's brown leather jacket on the back of one of the kitchen chairs. She fetched a glass, looked into the oven then banged its door shut.

"What would you like to drink?" she asked, not looking at me.

I heard a toilet flush, a door open and someone come out, whistling out of tune.

"Toby, Nuri. Nuri, Toby," was the extent of Mona's introduction.

I stood up and shook the man's hand.

"I've heard a lot about you," he said.

I looked at Mona, and she looked away.

"Finally Crumb thought it safe that we should meet."

"Toby, behave."

"Just glad to finally meet someone from your Egyptian odyssey," he told her. "We wondered if the old girl had deserted us."

After an awkward silence I asked, "Crumb?"

She blushed.

"I see," he said. "Hiding it from your fancy friends." Then to me he added, "It's her nickname, since she was a child."

He looked satisfied, smiling with his keen eyes on me.

"How's school?"

"I love it," I said and could not help looking again at Mona.

"Excellent," Toby said.

"He hates it," she told him.

"Don't believe her," I said. "I am having the time of my life. Really."

"It beats the City," he said. "I work in finance."

"And on which odyssey did you and Mona meet?"

"I like him," Toby told her and laughed. "University, we met at university. Many moons ago. Probably before your time."

"What was Mona like then?"

Toby was eager to tell me. He leaned forward and was about to speak when we heard Mona shout:

"Enough."

Toby looked at her, but she was looking at me. A silence as thick as sand fell now. Suddenly the music seemed very loud, and Mona must have thought so too, because she went to the stereo and turned it off.

"Don't worry," Toby told her. "I won't embarrass you."

"You already have," she muttered, and I pretended not to have heard that.

"She was, as sadly she remains, a genuine pain in the arse."

She threw a tea towel at him and covered her mouth.

"But, but," he laughed. "A diligent student notwithstanding." He pulled the tea towel off his shoulder. "So glad to have her back."

I stood up so violently that the chair fell against the wall behind me. Not knowing what to do or how to explain my abrupt movement, I looked at the time, at my father's old watch.

"I am sorry, so sorry . . . I must . . ."

I slung the bag over my shoulder.

"Where are you going?" she asked.

I tried not to look too long into her eyes: how ashamed and lost they seemed, how dark and small.

"I am already late."

"For what?" she said.

"I had promised a school friend I would stay over."

"But you . . . The dinner?" she said.

"Sorry."

"But when will you be back?"

"Tomorrow. Definitely."

Now I was winning; it felt like I was winning.

"But you can't just leave. And who is this friend, anyway?"

"Alexei," I said.

"But hasn't he left school?"

"He's in London, visiting."

"Give me his number. I need to know how to get hold of you."

"I don't have it. I will call as soon as I get there."

Toby placed his arm around her. "He's not a child," he told her.

They followed me to the door and stood waiting as the lift crept up. I stared at my shoes. I knew that she knew that I was lying, that there was no friend expecting me and that, more than anything else, I wanted to be expected, waited for, welcomed. Now her silence came to resemble a challenge. I must not turn back, I told myself. I must prove to her that I can do this. Tears filled my eyes. I fixed them on the lift door and prayed that neither of them would place a hand on my shoulder. The lift arrived and I quickly got in. After the doors shut I heard her say, "Call as soon as you get there."

And just like that I was out into the night again. The rain had stopped, but the air was colder. The dampness had gone through my coat. I trembled and told myself it was not fear. I was alone in London, but I could afford a hotel. After all, that is what people do, I told myself, when they have nowhere else to stay. And I had experience. Had I not countless times followed Father to the reception desk of some hotel in a foreign city? I recalled how he used to say, "I have a booking." And although I had no booking, it comforted me to imagine him there, beside me, just out of view to the left.

I found a hotel more quickly than I had anticipated, on the same street, perhaps six or seven doors down, overlooking the same canal. I knotted my scarf to hide the school tie.

With all the confidence I could muster I approached the reception and slowly lowered my bag.

"I would like a room, please. I don't have a booking."

He shot a glance beyond me.

"For one," I said, and, although his face remained uncertain, he pulled out a form and took my details.

"Do you have a preference which floor?" he asked.

I was not sure and could feel myself begin to sweat. Then I thought of the floor she lived on and said, "Fourth."

He asked for a deposit, and it was half of the money I had. Earlier that day at the bank I had imagined us going to Clarisse's for fondue and then on to the cinema, so I had withdrawn half of my monthly allowance.

I sat in the darkened room by the window and watched the light of the streetlamps play on the water. This was not Cairo, and the slim canal was certainly not the Nile, but I tried to imagine living here, seeing this view every day. Then I realized I was shivering. The cold had reached my bones and touched them. Mother used to run me a bath in winter. That is what I must do to kill the shiver, I told myself. I lay in the bathtub until the hot water cooled.

I left the bathroom light on and entered the cold sheets. Every time I heard someone come up the stairs my heart quickened. I was certain the footsteps were coming to my door, and only after they passed could I start breathing again. At one point I was convinced that one of the voices approaching was that of Toby. And when the woman beside him answered and she did not sound like Mona, I argued that perhaps that was how she spoke to him, that, like the tone she used to reserve for Father, she had one especially for Toby too.

The following day a fever set in. By eleven the receptionist called to ask if I intended to stay another night. "Yes," I answered, and that was that. An hour later I ordered soup and tea, and the receptionist hesitated before saying, "I will see what I can do." The man who delivered them kept looking around the room as I counted the money. By early afternoon I was wrapped in my coat again and making my way down the staircase. I walked to Mona's building and rang the bell. She answered quickly.

"It's me," I said.

"Where have you been?" she said, and pressed the buzzer.

When I got out of the lift I found her waiting.

"Where have you been?" she asked again and walked away into the flat. "I have been worried sick about you."

"But I told you I was staying with a friend."

"Yes, and you said you would call. You gave me a fright. What if something happened? And where is your bag?"

"At the hotel."

"What hotel?"

"The one I stayed at with Alexei. Here, on the same street."

Her face changed. Tears appeared, and she opened her arms and came toward me. She held me for a few seconds, then said, "Come, let's go," and we walked to the hotel. I was relieved when she said she would wait downstairs. I did not want her to witness the room, the messy bed. She paid the receptionist, and as we walked back to her building she handed me the deposit, then ran her fingers through my hair.

Neither of us mentioned Toby. I did not visit again until the summer before my final year at Daleswick, and then only for one night on my way to Heathrow and on to Tanzania, where my year spent a couple of months helping to build an orphanage. I sent her a postcard on which I wrote that I had never felt more at home than in Tanzania. I told her about a visit we had paid to the university of Dar es Salaam. I reminded her that I had only one year remaining before university and that I was still undecided where to go. But when she wrote back, she did not pick up on that; she did not say anything about wanting me to remain in England.

CHAPTER 29

In the end I chose a university in London. I got a flat in Holland Park, not too far from Little Venice yet not so close that I might be accused of intruding.

Occasionally I met Mona. These encounters usually started the same way. I would go to her flat and watch her hover nervously for a few seconds before she grabbed her handbag and keys and said, "OK, let's go." We would walk by the canal, then sit in a nearby pub named the Bridge House. I felt observed and suspected she did too.

"What did Father tell you about his work?"

"You know he never talked about that."

"But he must have told you something."

"Your father had a gift for secrets—his final act proves it." Then after a long silence she said, "He was fixated on that country. It was an obsession."

"It was a noble cause," I said because I did not like the word obsession. "He was very brave."

"Yes," she said. The agreement was genuine; it passed through her with unique gentleness.

Sometimes I would ask her to recall certain details from our last day in Switzerland, a country I had not returned to since Father's disappearance; as far as I knew, neither had she.

"Tell me again what the policeman said."

She would fidget. "Well, you were there, weren't you?"

"Who was it that called our room? Remember? After Hydar and Taleb?"

"No one called."

"They did. And I think in Athens you used the telephone again."

"Athens?"

"Yes, we transited there."

"I don't remember. It all passed in a panic."

× × ×

I kept a small radius of friends, mostly from university, with whom I shared what I imagined some siblings share: a warm alliance that still assured the necessary distance. We went to concerts, ate at restaurants, called one another on birthdays. They seemed quite satisfied with the admittedly little I was able to give. They did not know much about me except that I came from Egypt—a fact in itself untrue. A certain kind of English temperament suited me because I was never one given to confession. I did not dress as lavishly as Father yet avoided the deliberate casualness of the fashion of the time. When invited for supper at someone's home, I made sure my gifts were moderate: neither too plain nor too enthusiastic. I never professed any strong or unyielding opinions, unless it was the only way not to stand out. And whenever someone said something about how racist the English were or expressed, in that subtle way, self-satisfaction at the fact that they counted among their friends a dark-skinned Arab, I simply pretended, in the way one does when an old person farts out loud, that I had not heard.

I occasionally had a lover, but with each act of lovemaking the old guilt I had felt during that night with Mona all those years ago did not become lighter but almost worse. I remember one woman—Katharine was her name, an architect—who asked me why I had tears in my eyes. I, embarrassingly, said nothing, hoping she might mistake them for the emotions of a lover. More often than not these bouts of guilt manifested themselves in a cold aloofness that left the woman—usually still naked at this point—either offended or perplexed, in both cases requiring an explanation. The morning after I would feel the need to call Mona. Attempting to sound casual, I would tell her about a new play I had seen, a new restaurant I had discovered. Sometimes I would even find myself saying something like, "I think you and Toby would enjoy it."

I was twenty-four and had just earned a PhD in art history when, according to the rules of Father's will, I was free to do as I pleased. The papers Monsieur Hass posted a week after my birthday confirmed this: they declared that I was in full control of my inheritance. The options of where and how to live seemed infinite. I found no comfort in this.

I began to feel I had been neglecting my father. I saw him waiting in a windowless room. I obsessed about what I could do to find him. I dreamed of him often.

In one dream I am sitting on a bench, knowing he will come. Suddenly he is beside me. I do not know how, but we are the same age. There is something tragic about this fact. He is silent. He is wary of me. Perhaps, I hope from within the dream, one day I might put him at ease. In these dreams I am always the talkative one, like a nervous fellow train passenger. He hardly looks at me. Each time I see him I notice something else about him that has changed: the rhythm of his breath, the way an unpressed collar curls round his neck. In one dream he places a hand on my back, between the shoulder blades, and the heat of his palm bothers me, but I say nothing. Another time he is hungry. I break off pieces of cheese into my lap and feed him with my hand. In another dream he tells me, "I wish I had more world in the world." When I ask what he means, whether he means more children, he says nothing. I want to know how to comfort him. Then he says, "She whispers in my ear at times," and I know he means Mother. "Her voice. Her warm breath at my ear, across my neck." His cheeks turn red, like a young man's, like his face in that picture I keep, taken by my mother, when they were newlyweds. He touches my arm, and I think, happily, we have become friends. Then a tear that had slid down the side of my face dropped into the shell of my ear and woke me.

×　×　×

One morning I packed a small suitcase and flew to Geneva.

I left my bag at a hotel named Eden and went wandering the streets. It was ten years since I had last been in the city. The sun was out and, although it was the afternoon, it shone as pale as an early morning sun. I was walking down the Grand Rue when I began to feel myself relax. The shift in mood was as inexplicable as it was wonderful.

By nightfall I located the street, Rue Monnier, on which Béatrice Benameur had allegedly lived. The street name had been fixed in my memory since that December day ten years earlier when Hass had attempted to introduce us to the mysterious Swiss woman. It would not have been strange if the street had seemed smaller—as indeed most places one knew as a child do seem—but instead the tarmac was wider than I remembered it, the pavements on either side broader and the buildings taller and more dominant against the night sky. I stood on the opposite pavement from the arched building entrance that was flanked by those two hideous plaster cupids. I thought of what I might do if I saw her. I watched the windows. Only a few were lit. I took out the map and by the streetlight found the most direct route downtown—the way I suspected Father might have walked. I located what I surmised was the nearest tobacco shop and bought a packet of Dunhill, the brand of cigarettes my father smoked. The familiar flat pack fit perfectly in my shirt pocket.

For all I knew, Béatrice Benameur might have moved during the ten years—if indeed she ever lived there—but nonetheless I was so unsettled by having successfully located the building that after breakfast the following morning I wandered back to Rue Monnier. This time I had the courage to consult the names on the buzzers—why had I not done this the day before? Dread and excitement were in my throat. And there it was: "Mlle. BENAMEUR." I had to read it more than once. The name seemed oddly new, as if I had never seen it before.

Suddenly I needed to be out of the narrow maze of streets. After a couple of turns I found a café on one of the nearby avenues. At first the place seemed like any other, but then as soon as I sat down I became convinced that I had been there before, perhaps with my parents on one of the numerous visits we made to this city. I sipped the coffee quickly and left.

The avenue looked onto a park. I walked around it a few

times then sat on a bench. After a couple of hours I began to
feel calmer.

× × ×

I returned to the same café for lunch. I had been sitting
there in the corner for some time—doing what Mona used
to do, "polishing my French" on a copy of *La Tribune de
Genève*—when, after the lunchtime crowd thinned, I realized I recognized the woman in the tapered skirt sitting
by the window. Before I recognized her, I had taken note
of how she would bring one hand between her thighs
and clench it while still holding a cup of coffee close to
her mouth in the other hand, sometimes resting the rim on
her lower lip long after she had taken a sip. She looked like
Béatrice Benameur. I was still uncertain: was she really
the woman with whom Father had spent his last hours? It
was ten years later, and the newspaper photograph was
not very well printed. I wished I had brought the cutting
with me. But I was as familiar with that picture as if it really
were a picture of my own father. Looking at her now—
immaculately dressed, makeup so subtle and considered—
I could not move. She did not seem to have aged much in the
last ten years. It was as though no time had passed at all,
as though Father might still be lying in her bed or might
suddenly walk into the café and sit opposite her. I was
grateful for her beauty, pleased for him. I wanted to walk
over to her table, but I was gripped by the conviction that

any action I might take would cause the moment and its possibilities to vanish. Besides, what would I say? All I could do was watch her beyond the newspaper. She stood up to leave. This was my chance. But when she looked in my direction I lowered my eyes.

"A bientôt, Mademoiselle Benameur," the waiter said.

I paid and left. I caught a glimpse of her turning in to another street. I ran after her. I looked back and saw the waiter standing outside the café in his long white apron, perfectly pressed in large square creases, his eyes on me. I did not run after that and made sure my steps were measured. I turned the corner after her. She was already a good way down. I tried to run again, but my shoes hammered loudly on the cobbled stones. It did not matter; my steps were faster than hers, and eventually I was an arm's length away, inhaling deeply, trying to smell her. But I caught nothing, not even when she stopped to look at the time and I stood so close behind that, when I blew, the outer strands of her hair parted. She lit a cigarette and walked through the plume. I watched her cross the road. She rang the doorbell of an understated building that had a pale wooden door with a small brass plate. A Swiss flag hung from a mast at the second floor. The cloth was so large that its red corner brushed against the top of her head as she pushed the door and disappeared inside.

That night I could not sleep from the excitement, the possibilities. I decided that I would try to get to know her without revealing my identity. I was worried that if she knew who I was she would be frightened away, like she had been ten years earlier.

× × ×

The following day, walking across the Pont de la Machine under the white September sun, the lake opening and glittering toward the snow-patched mountains in the distance, I found a cluster of figures gathered, gloved hands on the railing, heads bent, a couple of them shouting instructions at the fully dressed man below who was desperately trying to climb out of the water.

He hugged the bridge column, managed to extract his torso from the fast current and then slipped again. He was looking desperately up at the bank beneath the bridge where I could see a woman kneeling over, her hair tied in a scarf as if she had just stepped out of a convertible. I could not see her face, but from the way she held her arm I suspected she had her hand against her mouth. His head was bobbing above the water. His nose began to bleed. He wiped it, threw his head back. For a moment his eyes looked up at us, but he seemed to take no notice of the anxious calls to hurry, to reach once again for the column, to not give up. His body was moving furiously beneath the water. No sooner had he brought his head upright than his lips and chin were covered in blood. He began another attempt at scaling the bridge. He slipped and splashed back into the waters. The woman under the bridge did not move.

"Call the fire brigade," one man shouted.

"We have," another told him. "A while ago."

"Why are they taking so long?" the woman behind me said so softly that I felt obliged to look back at her.

The man in the water was working hard now, a new strength in his arms. The column was less than a meter away. He took hold of it and managed to make it up to the first beam. He was now out of view. The water looked darker without him. Being against the railing, I leaned over like the others to see. Whenever someone from behind asked whether the man had made it, we ignored them. I kept my eyes on the woman. She was still on her knees, but her hand had now left her mouth and was stretched out as if she was saying, "Stay there." When he finally jumped onto the sloping bank, water jetting through the stitching of his black leather shoes, we all clapped. The woman opened her arms and the man fell into her, his head quickly finding her lap. She fingered his wet hair, combing it, tucking it behind his ears and, because from that angle she could not bend to kiss him, she pulled his palm to her face. She untied her scarf and collected it in a ball beneath his nostrils. Her hair relaxed into the air, as if it were breathing it, and fell thick and black. And now, as the distant siren grew nearer, the stillness of those around me seemed less an expression of concern and more a celebration. I walked hurriedly away toward the café, overwhelmed by a sudden feeling of reck-lessness and of hope.

CHAPTER 30

It was lunchtime, and the café was nearly full. The only free table was by the window. The waiter watched me from the doorway without speaking. Eventually he came to my table. I ordered the steak, rare, as I remembered Father liking it. I thought of him sitting in this restaurant, in one of his dark-gray suits. I wondered if I would be able to locate his tailor. I remembered how I used to sit on a stool in the shop, watching him being measured. Perhaps I could order a three-piece in the style he preferred, I thought. The lunch crowd left, and I was the only one in the place. Béatrice Benameur never came. At one point I had the idea that the waiter was on the telephone with her. As he talked he glanced over in my direction then turned his back, whispering, nodding. I became certain he was taking instructions. When he hung up I waved for the bill.

I went to my room and remained in bed until the following morning, hardly sleeping. I wondered how she would react if I were simply to ring her buzzer and introduce myself. I thought of calling Taleb and asking what he suggested I should do. I thought of calling Mona, asking her to come. At nine in the morning I finally telephoned the office of Monsieur Hass. I had been meaning to call him as soon as I arrived in Geneva but somehow had not been able to face it. I got no answer. I redialed every five minutes until, at around 9:45, his secretary answered.

"Did you call before?" she asked.

"No," I said.

She put me on hold, then returned to say, "Monsieur Hass would like you to come as soon as you are able. Can you come now?"

The ten years that had passed since I had last seen Charlie Hass had thinned his already slender frame; his suit hung a little loosely now. He seemed shorter somehow, and there was a slight hunch in the shoulders. His hair was no longer black. Thin strands clung to his scalp. But the most significant yet subtle change was in the eyes. They had become less certain, more wary. He seemed to have given way to the inevitability of his doubts.

We shook hands, then he held me by the shoulders.

He sat behind his desk and I in the small armchair opposite.

"You look like your father," he said. "You hold yourself in the same way."

The secretary's arm stretched beside me and set a coffee cup on the desk. Hass waited until she left.

"So what brings you to Geneva?"

"Just passing through. Thought I should show my face, say thank you."

"Everything is OK moneywise, I hope?"

I noticed a thin veil of moisture glistening on his brow. A new expression passed across his face then vanished.

"Living with his legacy, with what he had done, the path he had taken, must be difficult."

I was sure he took the silence that followed as agreement.

"But you must not blame him. He certainly did make difficult choices, but you must not judge him. You must put all that aside and be proud of his bravery, his single-mindedness. A lesser man, especially with his intelligence and means, would have walked away, lived a provincial life somewhere."

"I would not have minded that."

He did not respond, but the droplets of sweat on his brow swelled.

"I remember him mentioning a town in northern California, a place he liked. Yes, I remember it now. He was sitting where you are, in the same chair, and said, 'Charlie, I am thinking of taking my boy and moving to America. I have bought a place for the purpose. In Point Reyes.' 'Where is that?' I asked. 'Northern California,' he said and I could not restrain myself. I'm glad to say he laughed too. The thought of your father relaxing on a Californian beach! But I think he did feel torn, worried what his life might mean for you. Worried where things might end up. He was right to worry, of course."

We both were silent. Hass let out a heavy breath.

"I took him out after that for a wonderful lunch—your father was famous for his long lunches—and he never mentioned California again."

Suddenly everything in that room looked old, worn out: the desk and old sofa in the corner, Hass's suit.

He looked down at his fingers, which were long and thin, and spoke softly, as if to himself.

"He really was a great man."

I let my eyes rest on the gold irises linked round the inside lip of the small coffee cup. There was comfort in staring at the blackness of the coffee, the steam rising in gray breaths above the liquid.

"Whatever happened to Béatrice Benameur?"

His eyes here looked even more wary.

"Did you ever track her down again?"

"Yes. The years have been hard on her too."

"I would like to speak with her. After all . . ."

For some reason I could not complete the sentence.

"Of course. I'll try," he said gently into the silence. "Leave it with me."

I wrote down, slowly, the name of the hotel where I was staying, the room number.

× × ×

I descended the Old Town to the lake's edge and there sat on a bench. My mind set off imagining another possibility of myself: one who was more proactive, more courageous and more capable, one whose interrogations were less desperate and incomprehensible to himself. The shame and the regret nagged, and together they were as persistent as the cries of the seagulls that hovered now above the lake. The clouds were skipping fast. They cut the light into lines that traced the water and the craggy backs of the mountains that blocked the horizon. I felt dizzy, as if comprehending the scale of things for the first time and with it the vast yet intricate reality of the physical world and my precarious presence in it. I held my head and stared at the blades of grass at my feet. I counted the stitches round the leather of my shoes. I wanted this world to still. I wanted to fix it and be fixed within it. But everything was on the move, the clouds, the wind.

A boy was now sitting on the other end of the bench. How long had he been there? He watched me for a long time before he spoke.

"Are you sad?" he asked.

I tried to smile.

He looked down at his knees again. His legs were too short to reach the ground. Every so often he kicked the air. He turned around suddenly. How did he detect his mother approaching? She came and sat down between us, took out something wrapped in a paper bag and handed it to him. She took it back and peeled off the wrapping and handed it to him again. They sat in companionable silence, eating their sandwiches, his mother turning now and then to wipe the crumbs from his chin.

I left them and climbed up into the maze of streets of the Old Town. I walked fast until the steep roads slowed me down. Night fell like a shutter. There was no moon. The streetlamps were on. It must have rained, too, because the amber light was reflecting off the wet cobblestones. I touched my hair, and my palm shone. But the air was wonderfully mild, and I felt no need to button my jacket. The trees and bushes, swollen with late summer, released their scent. I was alone. The streets were deserted. I looked at the time— at the watch my father had last worn in this very same city. It was half past eleven. I had been walking for hours. The stone buildings stood dimly in the night, and, looking at them, I felt a deep longing to inhabit their rooms. To make love and eat and bathe and sleep in there, to quarrel and make promises, to sit with friends and talk into the night, to listen to music, read a book, write a letter, consider the position of a new object, watch flowers in a low vase, watch them at different times of the day, clip their stems and replace their water daily, move them away from a harsh light, a drafty passage, draw out their time. It was then that I heard a man calling me. How strange it was to hear my name echoing in the vacant street. Then the clatter of hoofs. I turned, expecting to see a horse's full and muscular chest approach. But I was mistaken. They were footsteps. Two people. One was Monsieur Hass. I would have recognized him sooner were he alone. He looked far more relaxed than when I had seen him earlier that day in his office. A strand of silver hair fell over his forehead. His arm was intertwined with that of a woman. She had on the same pencil skirt. When I recognized who she was I took a step back. It felt as if all the air had gone out of my lungs. I could not speak.

Béatrice Benameur extended her hand.

"I am so sorry." She paused. "But I am so pleased to meet you, finally." She placed her other hand on top of mine.

Yes, they were definitely tears.

"I saw you yesterday at the café," she went on, "but I didn't know who you were. Now Charlie tells me . . ."

Hass laughed. "She got the wrong idea, thought you were . . ."

She unhooked her arm, and that made him stop. She dabbed the place beneath her eyes with a piece of tissue paper folded into a small square.

"Can we walk together? I only live in the next street. You must have many questions," she said.

We walked, she on one side, I on the other, with Monsieur Hass in the middle. There were so many things I wanted to ask; so much was unanswered that I felt a sudden, terrible panic.

We reached her building, the one with the cupids. I wanted to ask her now why she had not opened up when Hass brought Mona and me to her door all those years ago. I wanted to know whether she really had been inside all along, perhaps on the floor behind the sofa, shutting her eyes tightly every time Hass pressed the loud buzzer.

We shook hands, and she placed her other hand on top of mine again. I realized she must have picked up the Arabic habit from my father.

"Please come up," she said. "I have always wanted to . . ."

Now that the moment I had longed for had finally arrived, I could not speak. In the silence that followed, Hass looked at her. He then nodded earnestly.

"There will be time," he said. "You are not leaving yet, are you?" When I did not respond, he said, "Good."

He followed her, which surprised me because, even though they had walked arm in arm, I was certain they were not lovers.

I could not bear the parting. I had to force myself back to the hotel.

CHAPTER 31

In the morning I telephoned Hass's office. His secretary put me on hold for a long time, then returned to say, "I'm sorry, I will have him call you straightaway." I remained beside the telephone. My heart quickened every time I heard the telephone downstairs ring, then the receptionist say, "Hôtel Eden, bonjour." Twenty minutes later he called back. I let the telephone ring three times before answering it.

"We need to talk. I need to explain. I will come to you. Can you meet in ten minutes?"

Fifteen minutes later he walked through the hotel lobby.

"After you," he said, placing a hand between my shoulder blades as we entered the same compartment of the revolving door.

After a few paces I stopped.

"How long have you known her?"

He lightly held my elbow. "Come," he said.

"Before or after the disappearance?" I asked, refusing to move.

"Before," he said softly, regretfully. "Please, come, I'll explain everything."

He took me to the café where I had first spotted Béatrice. The waiter greeted him then looked at me for a second too long before he led us to a table by the window that looked out onto the street. Hass slid a long thin finger round his collar.

"I did not mean for you to meet her like that."

He pushed himself to the edge of the seat and looked at his hands.

"You lied to us," I said.

Instead of protesting he said, "Yes, I did. But out of kindness. It would have been too much."

"I don't understand. And what did you mean yesterday when you said that she had got the wrong idea? Who is she? And how do you know her? And if you knew her, then why didn't you tell me or Mona?"

"Actually, I did too. I had misunderstood the situation entirely. You see, I have been concerned ever since a couple of days ago when she passed by to tell me that there was a suspicious man in the café, an Arab-looking man who pretended to be reading a newspaper. 'Did he follow you?' I asked. She said, 'Yes,' and that, the next day, the waiter told her, the Arab had come back and looked like he was waiting for her. This happened once before, you see, and the experience left her . . . Well, she was distraught, absolutely dis-

191

traught, of course. Who can blame her? And I worried for her and for myself; it seems the people who took your father would stop at nothing. Even after you visited my office yesterday I did not put two and two together. But how was I to know that the man she had encountered was you? So I told her not to visit the café again. And last night, when you saw us together, I was walking her home."

Then Hass looked down at his hands and smiled a sincere, affectionate smile.

"When we first saw you, she held tightly to my arm and said, 'That's him.' I laughed. 'That is Kamal's son,' I told her, and she could not stop looking at you. She wanted me to introduce you right there and then, but, like I said, I didn't want you to meet that way. So she insisted we follow you from a distance. At one point we were so close that we heard you talking softly to yourself. But then suddenly you seemed to remember something. You began walking quickly and after a few streets we lost you. We came upon you again by chance. You were standing in the middle of the empty street, looking up at the buildings. I could see her eyes well up. 'He's crying,' she said and pulled me toward you."

Hearing this account made me uncomfortable. I tried to look out of the window.

"I am sorry you had to meet her that way," he said and laughed a nervous laugh. "But to think she thought you were . . ."

"Who did she think I was?"

He rubbed his hand harshly over his mouth.

"Monsieur Nuri, I am sure they visited you too."

"Who?"

"Do you mean to tell me that in all of these years no one came to see you?"

"For God's sake, who do you mean and what did they tell her?"

The waiter arrived at our table, so Hass stopped before answering. The waiter kept his eyes on me as he placed the coffee cups on the table.

"Do you know who this is?" Hass asked him.

The waiter looked apprehensive.

Hass went on, "It's Kamal Pasha's son."

The man's face changed. He looked at Hass for confirmation, and Hass raised his eyebrows and nodded. The waiter held out his hand, and I took it.

"Pleasure, pleasure," the waiter said.

"His only son," Hass said, as if he was remembering that fact for himself.

"Odd that you should come to the same café," the waiter said. "You felt him, monsieur, you felt him in the air."

I looked at Hass, and he explained: "Your father used to come here a lot."

"Really?"

"Yes," the waiter said. "Every morning. He used to live nearby, you know, and—"

"Enough of that now," Hass cut him off.

"Well, you are very welcome, monsieur, very welcome indeed," he said and shook my hand again.

After a short silence Monsieur Hass spoke.

"I have known Béatrice all my life. And, yes, I did hide that from you. But it would have been too difficult then for her and for you—particularly for Madame Mona—to meet."

He leaned back in his chair.

"You see, most men spend a lifetime trying to understand their fathers."

I was certain he had rehearsed that last line; it seemed to come from nowhere.

"In my case, there was no more mysterious a man than my father. He was the old-fashioned sort. Loving, but formal. Died when I was young. But I shouldn't think I would have felt different if he were still alive."

"My father and I were very close."

"Of course you were."

How did we end up in this place, I wondered, where he was pretending to tolerate my illusions?

"But the facts of a man's life," he went on, "tell much more than his presence. I need to tell you about Béatrice. You don't know who she really is or what she meant to your father. And when you know you will understand my actions."

"What was she doing there, anyway? It's very suspicious. And the fact that you lied to us makes it more so."

Hass turned to me with a serious look.

"You need to talk to her," he said. "Enough time has passed. She meant a great deal to your father and had nothing to do with his disappearance. She has suffered deeply, and silently, ever since it happened."

Then, after a long pause, he said, "What is it that makes some men unsuitable for married life? To some it's a comfort, to others a prison. And why are some content with one woman while others are not? These are stupid questions."

"I am relieved you think so."

"But the truth is, your father had lovers. However, with Béatrice, things were more complicated. I can say, without any doubt, that your father loved her. I would be very surprised, if he is still alive, if he is not still in love with her. It was very powerful. And together they had a life here, you see, in this city, which resembled a normal life, a life like any other married couple, one, I suspect, not too dissimilar from the life you and your mother shared with him in Cairo."

The ants were now all over my body. I wanted to leave. But then he spoke again.

"Something occurs between a man and a woman that no one can access." He looked out onto the street. "A secret that even they might never know. Here she comes," he said, and we both watched Béatrice cross the road. "Be tender," he whispered, and I found myself whispering back: "Don't worry."

× × ×

Béatrice Benameur walked into the café and sat beside Hass.

"I will leave you two to talk," he said, standing.

"Can you not stay?" she said.

195

He smiled at her in a way, I suspected, he reserved only for those with whom he was most intimate.

We watched him leave. He waved as he walked past.

"He is a good man. Can be overprotective. Ever since we were children he has been like this. Did he tell you? We are cousins."

"I see."

There is a moment when a deer sees its hunter and knows him. That was how Béatrice Benameur looked at me now. I recognized in her something of myself. We were the survivors, those fated to remain behind. She looked away, and I studied her features. Time had cut lines into a face that was undoubtedly still beautiful. I imagined how she and Father might look now sitting side by side, growing old in a city in which one could take many things for granted.

"There isn't a day that I don't think of him," she said. "He passed through my fingers. I feel responsible. As if I had dropped him."

I bit hard because my teeth were chattering. Was she the first person Father had telephoned the day Mother died? I would have forgiven him. I wondered what he was to her, what she called him, if they had nicknames for each other.

"In my mind," I said, "I never have him whole. I am always standing too close to take him in properly."

Then there was a long silence, and I felt I had said too much.

"They came in so quietly while we were asleep. I still don't know how they managed to break in without making a sound. I am such a light sleeper. Your father used to tease me; he would say a cloud passing over a full moon would wake me. When I woke up they were right there, a couple standing at the foot of the bed. I could not see their faces because the moonlight shone through the window behind them. The slowness of it. I turned to wake Kamal, but he was already up. I remember thinking: how did he know they were coming? He was sitting up in bed and looked like he had been waiting. I tried to scream but couldn't. By now I could make them out: a man dressed in a suit, almost smiling, and a woman standing beside him. She seemed panicked, really tense, and was shouting at her partner; he, on the other hand, looked like he had done this many times before. The man said something in Arabic, and Kamal began to get dressed. I started shouting, but none of them, not even Kamal, flinched. The woman pulled out a gun with a silencer, and I stopped. Her hands were trembling, I remember that. They held him by each arm and walked him out. He did not take his eyes off me. I can still see his face, turned back. I see it in dreams, and I see it when I am awake. I walked around the room. I didn't know what to do. Then I called Charlie; Kamal said that if anything ever happened I should call Charlie first. He asked me to wait twenty minutes before calling the police. When I asked why, he just repeated that I must wait at least that long. I understood when a journalist friend of his arrived five minutes before the police. Charlie's idea was that the more coverage the kidnapping got stressing the political angle—that an ex-minister and prominent dissident was snatched on Swiss soil—the more chance there was of finding Kamal. Of course I didn't want to be splashed across the tabloids, but I was glad to do it, because if the police had got there first the whole thing would have been hushed up in a minute." After a short pause she asked, "What do you think happened to your father?"

I did not know how to answer. The truth is, I don't believe Father is dead. But I don't believe he is alive either.

She took out a photograph from her handbag and placed it in front of me. Father standing on a corner pavement, the cobbled street falling steeply behind him, then elbowing right. His arms hang slightly away from his torso, sleeves rolled up. His eyes have a hint of bewilderment. They know. The cheeks, too, know: sunken and a shade darker. And in the shirt pocket there is the top of a cheap pen. He looks like a schoolteacher. He looks wary, ready.

"The Place du Bourg de Four, the day before it happened," she said and looked at me. "We were walking, and I thought I must take a photograph. Strange, because I never was one for taking pictures. But there was something peculiar about that day. You could feel it pass. You can keep it," she said, and then the tears came.

I rescued one hand.

"I should not cry. You lost so much more."

I wanted to ask about the blood on the pillow, the broken lamp shade, the signs of resistance reported in *La Tribune de Genève*. But then, looking out of the window, she said, "I hate this city, all the muck it gathers."

CHAPTER 32

That afternoon I located the spot on the Place du Bourg de Four and stood facing the same direction Father faced, toward the blinking shutters that overlooked the Rue Saint-Léger. I thought perhaps I should ask one of the passersby to take a picture of me in the same spot. They would have had no reason to suspect anything unusual. After a quarter of an hour, I put the camera away and walked on.

Béatrice had given me her number, but I wondered whether another conversation only a couple of hours after our meeting in the café would be too much for both of us. I stopped at a public telephone and, without knowing what I was going to say, I dialed her number. She answered.

"Can I stop by?" When she did not respond, I said, "I want to see where it happened."

"Of course."

I pressed the buzzer, and she answered immediately.

Standing in front of the apartment, I heard her light feet almost run to the door. She opened it and stood to one side. I could smell perfume. She pointed to the kitchen, where a newspaper was spread on a rectangular table that stood against the wall, a cup with something steaming beside it. The sun dappled through the yellowing leaves of a tree that reached above the window. When she saw me hesitate, she said, "Are you sure you want to?"

"Yes."

I followed her to the bedroom. The same window. I walked around the bed to where I had always imagined he was when it happened. I pressed my hands into the mattress. I sat down, my back to her. The bedside table had nothing on it. A biography of our king and Philip K. Hitti's *History of the Arabs* stood alone on a shelf on the wall. I lay down, still dressed in my coat and shoes. Only then did I realize she had left the room. I felt my body sink into the bed. The ceiling was perfectly white. There was not a crack or speck or insect or cobweb. I shut my eyes.

I found Béatrice in the kitchen, her eyelids red. She stood up when she saw me and opened a hand toward the opposite chair. I sat down and watched the watery light pass through the leaves behind her. There was no need to talk.

x x x

Some minutes later she spoke.

"Everything you see we picked together. When we first moved here he insisted we even paint the walls ourselves."

I could not imagine my father doing that.

"He was so excited: picking out the colors, learning how to use the roller. He made me laugh."

I looked around the room at the walls.

"I had some of the gentlest, most beautiful times with him. I wanted it to last forever."

After a long silence I felt I needed to say something good.

"Two days ago I watched a man almost drown. He was bleeding from the nose. He struggled with all his strength. I was certain he wasn't going to make it. But he did."

When I looked at her she smiled.

"How's your stepmother?" she suddenly asked.

I was surprised by the question as much as by my frank response:

"Things between us have become very complicated."

"You need to be gentle with her. Her situation is more difficult. She must know that your father married her because of you. He always punished himself, wishing he were a better father. He used to say he loved you so much he froze around you. At first he thought Mona might be good for you because he saw how fond you both were of each other."

× × ×

Later that day Charlie Hass called my hotel.

"Monsieur Nuri, I must thank you. You have made Béatrice happy for the first time in a long time. I do hope you will remain in touch."

CHAPTER 33

I flew back to London and immediately went to see Mona. I told her I had been in Geneva and I had news. Toby had lost his job and moved in with her. She threw her keys into her handbag and I followed her out. She walked half a step ahead, her boots angry at the pavement. We sat at a small table in a dark corner of the same pub, the Bridge House. She had her back to the wall. The light from behind me powdered her face white.

"I met Béatrice."

"Oh yes? What did you find out? God, you should have called. Did you think she had had a tip-off? I wish I could have been there. She must have been paid an awful lot of money to sleep with your father."

I did not know how to answer. It was as if she was not really talking to me at all. Just reasoning it all out.

"They were lovers. For a long time, Mona. He was in love with her. It wasn't only that night. They had been together for years."

Her faced seemed to collapse. The corners of her mouth twitched, but she said nothing. I suddenly had the strange realization that I was almost enjoying myself. I did not mind telling her. I almost wanted to see how far I could push her. Then it was as if she was mustering every part of herself to speak:

"Oh, of course she told you that. Wouldn't want to seem like a whore to Kamal Pasha's charming son. That's hardly a surprise."

Along with the word surprise, specks of saliva shot out into the light like fine pieces of broken glass.

I felt obliged to defend her—the woman my father loved last.

"She wasn't like that at all," I said. When she did not speak I felt I could go further. "He clearly loved her. He was good to her. She knew him better than we did."

"You go tell that to Naima," she spat.

"What does Naima have to do with any of this?"

"Oh, please, don't tell me you never suspected it. I mean, you must have looked at yourself in the mirror and wondered . . . I mean, look at the color of your skin, for God's sake. And how she always fussed over you."

I thought of running. I remembered how Naima would take my mother's place by my bedside whenever I was ill. And how once, when I was feverish, Mother stepped to one side when Naima walked in breathless. The next time I looked up, Mother was gone. I confronted her about this. It was late in the evening; the sky had but a thin veil of light. I babbled and stuttered, and she held me and said, "I know, it breaks my heart too. But we mustn't see it this way. We are all lucky. We must count ourselves lucky," and she began to kiss each hand, each cheek, my forehead. And, as was often the case with Mother, whether naturally or by sheer force, she managed to steer the conversation away from painful subjects. She stood up and, doing a sort of Charlie Chaplin impression, twisted an invisible mustache and started to recite some lines by al-Jahiz about the appropriate manners a man must show his donkey.

I hated Mona at that moment. I hated her spite and anger and sadness. I was determined to hold on to my composure. I looked at her. The skin around her neck looked iridescent in the light, her lips a careless dab of paint. She shut her eyes and pressed the tips of her fingers to the bridge of her nose. Then she sighed, and her hand was around her drink once more. All but a transparent coin of ice had melted. Without taking a sip, she let go of the glass and rubbed her hand on her thigh. I wondered if she needed money.

"I look like my great-grandfather," I said after the long silence. "That's why I'm darker."

But these words left a desperately hollow feeling. She looked up at me but did not speak. I stood up. She reached for her bag, and we both walked out of the pub and into the bright afternoon.

"I must go," she said.

"Me too."

She walked off, and I turned and walked away in the other direction. As soon as I turned the corner I vomited onto the pavement. Tears covered my eyes. An old lady with a dog stopped to ask if I was all right. I managed to nod, and she walked on. That was the last time I saw Mona.

x x x

One night, a couple of months later, I found myself standing again in the rain, on the opposite side of the canal from her flat, facing the lit window. I felt a fire in me, and it was not good. I asked myself what would help and could find no answer. Not even possessing her would have done it. I watched her shadow pass across the ceiling of her bedroom. I knew I had to leave London then.

CHAPTER 34

The plane landed in Cairo just as day was breaking. When I sat in the back of the taxi, I was surprised how ready the old address was on my tongue: "Twenty-one Fairouz Street, Zamalek." A thin mist waxed the warming, empty streets. Memories returned. I remembered how my mother used to pass the brush through her hair, unhurriedly and away, like someone pushing away bad news. Then I recalled standing on my knees on a bed in a cabin aboard the *Isis* as it made its way up the Nile and deeper into the continent, combing Mona's hair. Everything I loved and all of what was lost was once here. And now I was arriving into absence, after everyone had gone.

Deeper into the city, the streets tangled. Cairo was almost fully awake. I tried not to let the swollen pavements, the choked lanes, unnerve me. It was as if, in the eleven years I had been gone, a terrible truth had disquieted the city of my childhood.

And here were the familiar streets of the river island district of Zamalek. All of us—Mother, Father and even Mona—were everywhere I looked.

When we reached Fairouz Street I could see Am-Samir, the porter, sitting on the steps of the building, facing the road and the Nile beyond. There were mornings in London when I used to wake up agitated by the possibility of his dying or moving away. He had been a constant figure in the desolate landscape. I had not told him I was coming. I wanted to keep open the option of turning back. He did not recognize me when I got out of the taxi and started to un-load the suitcase. But how could he have recognized the fourteen-year-old boy I was in the twenty-five-year-old man I had become? He looked older. The strong trunk of his neck had withered, and his Adam's apple protruded more prominently and seemed as delicate as a bird's skull. His mustache had thickened with white, wiry hairs. It was as if the years had gathered their forces around him and were now a company and a comfort. He looked at me with a kind of benign curiosity.

I had kept the scantest correspondence with Am-Samir over the years: always brief and concerning the upkeep of the family apartment. The man could not, as the expres-sion here went, disentangle a line, and so he dictated his brief letters to his son Gamaal, who was only a year older than me.

As soon as Gamaal had learned how to read and write Am-Samir pulled him out of school to sit on the rickety wooden bench in the drafty entrance. I remember how Gamaal used to sit there, watching me with a kind of bewildered, envious curiosity whenever I ran down the stairs to catch the school bus or, in the late afternoons, when I would walk out holding my mother's hand as we strolled together up the corniche. And he watched me when I returned from horseback riding or tennis or croquet too, and would tap my shoulder nervously and hand me a ball or riding whip that I had accidentally dropped in the hallway.

In his letters Am-Samir would always inquire, through his son: "How is your health, Nuri Pasha? When will we see you again?" and would always end with: "We will never forget your parents." The last line sometimes read like an accusation that my absence was a betrayal of their memory. At other times it flattered me. These inquiries, accusations or compliments were always met by a reserve that I regretted as soon as I posted yet another letter. But I avoided any guilt by thinking these evasions were necessary given the reader, Gamaal, who stood between us. But now there I was, and there he was, with no one in between. I stood on the pavement, looking at him. He walked over to me, checked my face and then wrapped his arms around me. He smelled as dry and clean as plowed earth. He placed his coarse hand on my cheek, patted my head although I was now taller than he was. I could see tears in his gray eyes.

"What good news," he said. "What good news! Gamaal," he called. "Look who's here! Sir, we have missed you. Now happy days are back. Look how you have grown."

I could not stop smiling.

Gamaal stood behind his father. He looked more circumspect, but the eager envy had gone from his eyes. No doubt, one by one, he had let go of his expectations.

I left father and son arguing over who was going to carry the suitcase. Gamaal got hold of the handle first.

"Move," Am-Samir ordered. "I have been waiting for this day."

"But your back?"

"Ten times stronger than yours."

× × ×

The lift seemed smaller. I pressed the number three. The feeling cast itself like a fisherman's net around me: I was finally where I ought to be. After all, if Father returned, where else would he go but home?

Inside the apartment, I stood by the window and looked out at a view that had once been as familiar as my own reflection: the shoulder of the island nudging the river and the far bank bending a little in agreement. The wind was strong. It brought with it the sounds of the city.

"If you had warned us . . . Pointless otherwise to keep

clean an apartment not in use, don't you agree, Nuri Pasha?" Am-Samir let go of the suitcase, placing his hand against his lower back. "Can't quite believe my eyes. You have cheered us up, really, Pasha."

I thanked him.

"Naima will be happy," he said. "There isn't a month, I tell you, where she doesn't pass by to ask about you, I swear. In the early days she would come every other day. Poor girl, she never really found her feet."

"Where is she now?"

"She hasn't settled, Pasha. Every few months she moves to another family." He looked at my suitcase. "Is this the entire luggage? Shall I put it in the bedroom? I hope this doesn't mean you will be leaving soon?"

"No," I said. "The rest of my things will arrive this week. I will stay in a hotel until then."

"That's excellent news. I will have the place sparkling. And with joy, Pasha, I swear, with joy." He picked up the suitcase. "I will stop a taxi. The best car in Egypt."

He left, and after a few minutes I followed him.

"I will see you in a week," I said, getting into the cab.

"Everything will be ready," Am-Samir repeated, Gamaal standing behind him. And only after the taxi drove off did I remember that I should have given him some money. But I felt too embarrassed to return.

"Where to?" the driver asked.

I could only recall the name of one hotel:

"Magda Marina."

"Where is that?"

"Agamy Beach."

He laughed, but when he saw in the rearview mirror that I was not joking, he said, "But that's in Alexandria."

We set off on the three-hour drive. For the first time in years I felt good.

CHAPTER 35

A miracle that I managed to retrace my steps, and a miracle still that the Magda Marina had survived the relentless development inflicted on the coast. The 1960s southern Mediterranean architecture of the hotel, which had seemed naïvely optimistic, now struck me as elegantly old-fashioned. The same cropped lawns snaked around the same mirror-fronted concrete-box rooms. The same mock-Moorish tiles round the rectangular pool. I found the palm tree where I had sat all those years ago. The trunk had widened, and the canopy had climbed up too far for its shade to have much effect.

It was autumn, and the hotel was nearly empty. I could not remember the number of our old room, the room where Father and I used to stay, and so the receptionist guided me to the pool from where I was able to point it out.

"But that is a twin?"

"I know."

"Have you stayed there before?" he asked, walking back.

"When I was a boy. Many years ago."

He smiled at me.

When I had finished checking in, the bellboy, who waited eagerly to one side, led the way to the room. He took quick, short steps that suggested my bag was much heavier than it was.

I unpacked and went immediately to the sea. I swam so far out that I could no longer see land. I floated in the breathing silence. The water was so still and calm that I was not entirely certain which way was back. Suddenly I became conscious of how cold the water was. I began swimming, my face in the water, and tried not to get too nervous. After a few strokes I looked up and could see the thin sliver of land bobbing on the horizon.

× × ×

After lunch I telephoned Am-Samir.

"She just missed you," he said.

"Who?"

"Naima, Pasha, Naima. God in His grace. She passed by shortly after you drove off. The coincidence! She found us cleaning. 'Nuri Pasha is back,' I told her. She didn't believe me. Gamaal convinced her."

"Where is she now?"

"Cleaning the flat. She kicked us both out. You know what she's like," he said, laughing.

I lay in the curtained coolness of the room, on the bed where my father had slept, and paged through the newspaper, tilting it slightly, as he used to do, toward the lamp.

× × ×

The next few days were very much the same. My keenness for the sea persisted. I ate well. And slept even better. But as the days passed I began to long to get back to the Cairo apartment, to see Naima again. When the day came for me to return I felt sharply nervous. By the time the taxi entered the thick traffic of the city the nervousness turned to excitement.

I found the flat clean, both the beds made, and was hit by the smell of the food I used to eat as a child. New shelves had been put up in the hall, and my books were unpacked and ordered neatly on them. Many of the spines were upside down.

"Naima has just gone to the shops," Am-Samir said. "Any minute now she will be back. She is very happy, Pasha. Cooking a feast. Your favorite: stuffed grape leaves. See how we remember?"

I tried to ignore how violently my heart was beating.

I do not know how long she had been standing there. She was older, tears clinging to her eyelids like diamonds. I hugged her. She kissed my hand, front and back, pulled me down to kiss my forehead. I could not stop smiling. When she saw my face, she plunged herself into my chest and wept silently.

Am-Samir, too, was tearful, slapping one hand over the other and repeating, "How gracious is the Lord."

Gamaal stood to one side, his hands locked behind his back.

I had come home to servants.

I insisted that they eat with me. Gamaal said it was not possible. Am-Samir looked at him as if hoping his son was wrong.

"What then," I said, "you expect me to eat alone?"

They sat with me but hardly ate.

When Am-Samir and Gamaal left and Naima and I were alone, the silences assumed a new quality. Every time she finished asking if I wanted tea or coffee or what I would like tomorrow for breakfast, lunch, dinner, what dishes I missed most—"Do you remember my molokhia? You used to love my molokhia with stuffed pigeon"—and after every reply I made, it seemed that we were each slowly returning to the chain of our private thoughts. What I knew—and preferred that I did not know—could not be uttered. It was impossible to change our shared history, to be mother and son in the clear light of day. And this was not a hindrance, this impossibility—more a mercy.

Before she left on her long commute home, she showed me what she had done. While I was at the Magda Marina she had arranged all of Father's clothes in such a way that they now occupied only half of his wardrobe. She began unpacking my clothes. She hung the trousers and jackets opposite his suits. She stacked my underclothes beside his old, yellowing ones. She placed each one of my socks, with the tenderness of someone sowing seeds, in with the black, stone-like balls of Father's silk socks.

And that close photograph that Mother took of herself, the one that she had placed on the wall of my old bedroom only days before she passed away, was now standing on Father's bedside table. I was happy to leave it there.

Somehow Naima had assumed that I would take my father's room, sleep in his bed. And I did.

CHAPTER 36

Naima came every day. She labored over each meal, cooking enough to feed a family.

"The more mouths you feed, the more blessed your home will be," she would say.

She sent the leftovers to Am-Samir and the drivers who lingered downstairs.

The windows sparkled, and the floors gleamed. The laundry basket hardly spent a night full. She insisted on washing everything by hand, because "soapy clothes are bad for your skin." She would sit cross-legged on the tiled floor of the windowless laundry room and say, with raw mother-liness, as her unhappy hands kneaded the garments I had worn only the day before, "I don't care what you say, machines don't rinse properly." Her hands were covered in maps of pale scars from the repeated peeling over the years.

I bought her rubber gloves, but she never wore them, not even when bleaching the whites.

"You've spent too long abroad," she would say, laughing away my concern.

Every time I looked down I found a newly pressed shirt, the buttons marching up to my neck like the bolts of an ancient piece of armor. And if I dared pour myself a glass of water or attempt to make a cup of tea she would shoo me out of the kitchen.

× × ×

One evening, as she was preparing supper and repeating, "You won't believe what I made," the doorbell rang, slowly, with a long gap between rings. I did not leave Father's study, which had become my refuge, particularly during these evening hours. I could hear Naima welcoming warmly, then the soft utterances of a deep, masculine voice. When I walked out I saw, standing opposite her, with his back to me, a man dressed in a smart suit. He turned around, and I saw the familiar, gentle face of our old driver, Abdu. His tightly curled hair was powdered white; otherwise, his Nubian face was pretty much unaltered.

"See how lucky you are?" he said to Naima after embracing me.

Naima held her hands tightly against her stomach, shielding that permanently damp patch on her dress, the place where she leaned against the kitchen sink. She gave a shy smile, looked proud.

"I swear, God loves you," he told her. "Oh, yes," he went on. Then he looked at Naima, and at first I could not understand the meaning of his gaze. But then his eyes welled up. "Didn't I tell you everything would turn out all right?" he said. He took her by the ear. "And I had to hear it from others. God forgive you for keeping such good news to yourself."

She smiled so broadly that her brown teeth showed.

I took him to the study. He stood in front of the framed photographs on the shelf, those that were there from before, and the ones I had added since my return. He paused in front of each one before moving sideways, punctuating the silence with: "Welcome back, Pasha."

He refused to eat with me, and I was not quite ready for him to leave.

"You know," I said, "I haven't been down to see the old wagon yet."

He laughed. "You're still holding on to it? It's a fine car."

"Shall we go see it?" I said, and, after a slight hesitation, he stood up.

He was now working for the Ministry of Foreign Affairs.

"But I am semi-retired. They only call me when a foreign dignitary is visiting," he said proudly.

I nodded, my eyes on the fat knot of his tie. It was a pale purple with tiny white dots.

When we were beside the car, his pager beeped. He stood to one side with his back to me. Am-Samir, who had followed us down, began stripping off the dusty gray cover.

The old metal shone when he rubbed it with his palm. The wheels were entirely flat. I sat in the front passenger seat, where Father used to sit, particularly when he was riding alone with Abdu. The familiar smell of the leather made it seem as if the car had been holding on to the memory.

I watched Abdu. There was something unsettling about how well he had survived the tragedy: his fine suit, shiny black shoes, his confidence.

× × ×

It took a good month before the old telephone line was reconnected. I called Taleb in Paris and left a message on his answering machine. He called back and immediately, without saying hello, said, "Bizarre to be dialing the old number again."

We both tried to laugh.

"Hold on," I said. "There's someone here who wants to talk to you." I handed Naima the telephone.

"Who is it?" she whispered.

"Taleb."

"Taleb who?" Then she remembered and took the receiver.

I watched as her face smiled and reddened. She scratched repeatedly at a spot on the kitchen counter with her thumbnail.

When I took back the telephone Taleb was silent a second too long.

"God bless you," he said, and stopped. "You are a decent

fellow, Nuri." The timbre of his voice deepened. Then it changed. He told me about a call he had received from Mona. "She was terribly worried. Had no idea where you had disappeared to."

"What did you tell her?"

"What do you mean, what did I tell her? I told her you are in Egypt, of course. I can't believe you didn't tell her yourself." When I did not respond he said, "You must call her."

But I did not call her.

A few days after my conversation with Taleb, the telephone rang and I heard Naima say, "But I swear we have missed you, madam; the whole country misses you. And your Arabic is still good, mashallah."

Naima stuck her head into the study and whispered, even though the telephone was all the way by the kitchen, "It's Madam Mona, calling from England."

"Tell her I have stepped out," I said.

She hesitated, then went back to the telephone.

× × ×

I waited a week then telephoned. She answered after the first ring. Instead of reproaching me for leaving without informing her, she surprised me with a warmth I had not known from her for many years.

"I am so glad to hear your voice," she said. "How is Cairo? Please tell me. So good to speak to Naima the other day. She sounds good. And so do you."

A couple of days later she called.

"I've been thinking. Perhaps I could visit. It has been a long time."

"Yes," I said, hearing the detachment in my voice.

"Over the Christmas holidays, maybe?"

I did not respond.

"Will you be there?"

"I am not sure."

I was surprised by how vulnerable she sounded from this distance.

She continued to call every so often. She was working in one of the departments at Selfridges. And would say things like: "I enjoy it. The people are nice."

By November she began offering dates for when she might visit. My lack of enthusiasm probably made her as uneasy as it made me. The gaps between her calls increased until she stopped calling.

CHAPTER 37

One evening, after Naima had left for the day, I found myself taking out one of Father's suits. I buried my face in the jacket. I put it on, but it held my shoulders and chest too tightly. I felt constricted by it. The sleeves hung horribly short above the wrists. I never knew clothes could shrink so much from lack of wear. The suit might have fit the fourteen-year-old boy I was when I last saw my father, when my head barely reached his shoulder. I unfolded the underclothes. Once as white as salt, they were now stained unevenly to-bacco brown. The elastic that once held his waist was entirely gone, the band as hard as dried meat, and the double stitching round the neck and arms of the T-shirts had snapped between the loops.

I could not sleep.

I tried on more of his clothes. The tweed suit fit, albeit

stiffly. When I pushed my arms forward I could feel the fabric stretch a little. Perhaps if I wear it often, I thought, it will gradually return to its original size. I found his old raincoat, the one that used to hang behind the door to the study. It, too, seemed to have shrunk, but I was able to button it all the way up. I put my hands in his pockets. He had neglected to empty them. There was a crumpled-up tissue in one, a half-used tube of peppermints in the other. I put them back. I tied the belt around my waist the way he used to do. He will need a raincoat when he comes back. This might still fit him. I returned it to its place.

November 2010, London

ACKNOWLEDGMENTS

I would like to thank the following people: Mary Mount, Susan Kamil, Noah Eaker, Venetia Butterfield, Kevin Conroy Scott and Zoë Pagnamenta.

Devorah Baum, Andrea Canobbio, Keren James, Peter Hobbs, Lee Brackstone, Carole Satyamurti, Charles Arsène-Henry, Hazem Khater, Andrew Vass, Roger Linden and Jalal Mabrouk Shammam.

Dr. Mia Gray, Professor Dame Marilyn Strathern, Peter Sparks and the faculty of Girton College, University of Cambridge. Beatrice Monti della Corte of the Santa Maddalena Foundation. Thea and Robyn Pender and Hephzibah Rendle-Short.

Jaballa Hamed Matar, Fawzia Mohamed Tarbah, Ziad Jaballa Matar and Mahmoud Abbas Badr.

And, most of all, Diana.

H.M.

HISHAM MATAR was born in New York City to Libyan parents and spent his childhood first in Tripoli and then in Cairo. His first novel, *In the Country of Men*, was published in 2006 and was shortlisted for the Man Booker Prize, the Guardian First Book Award, and the National Book Critics Circle Award. It won six international literary awards, including the Commonwealth Writers' Prize Best First Book award for Europe and South Asia, the Royal Society of Literature Ondaatje Prize, and the inaugural Arab American Book Award. It has been translated into twenty-eight languages. Hisham Matar lives in London.

ABOUT THE TYPE

The text of this book was set in a Monotype face called Bell. The Englishman John Bell (1745–1831) was responsible for the original cutting of this design. The vocations of Bell were many—among others, bookseller, printer, publisher, type founder, and journalist. His types were considerably influenced by the delicacy and beauty of the French copper-plate engravers. Monotype Bell might also be classified as a delicate and refined rendering of Scotch Roman.